LOGAN'S CHOICE

LOGAN'S CHOICE

Frank Bonham

Chivers Press
Bath, England

G.K. Hall & Co.
Waterville, Maine USA

This Large Print edition is published by Chivers Press, England, and by G.K. Hall & Co., USA.

Published in 2001 in the U.K. by arrangement with the author c/o Golden West Literary Agency.

Published in 2001 in the U.S. by arrangement with Golden West Literary Agency.

U.K. Hardcover ISBN 0-7540-4665-6 (Chivers Large Print)
U.K. Softcover ISBN 0-7540-4666-4 (Camden Large Print)
U.S. Softcover ISBN 0-7838-9567-4 (Nightingale Series Edition)

The text of this Large Print edition is unabridged.
Other aspects of the book may vary from the original edition.

Set in 16 pt. New Times Roman.

Printed in Great Britain on acid-free paper.

British Library Cataloguing in Publication Data available

Library of Congress Cataloging-in-Publication Data

Bonham, Frank.
Logan's choice / Frank Bonham.
p. cm.
ISBN 0-7838-9567-4 (lg. print : sc : alk. paper)
1. Yaqui Indians—Fiction. 2. Large type books. I. Title.
PS3503.O4315 L6 2001
813'.54—dc21 2001039174

CHAPTER ONE

Yaqui weather, Tom Logan's father used to call it—the first scorching days of spring. Hot blue skies stretched over the broken hills and winding river valleys; above the mountains black thunderheads gathered, illuminated by flashes of lightning. Soon the warm rains would come to soak the dry soil, and the dun-colored hills would be tinged with green.

Yaqui weather. Any time after March, when the farms and cattle ranches of the Mexican border began hiring for the summer work, Yaqui soldiers, who a week ago had been setting bloody ambuscades for harried Mexican army patrols began moving north, seeking work. By twos and threes, elusive as smoke, hundreds of tall, dark-skinned Indians in the garments of Mexican farmers stole down the Santa Cruz River toward Tucson.

In the fall, having earned enough money to keep their three-hundred-year war going a little longer, they returned to the mountains of Sonora.

But a rancher never saw them—not unless they knew and trusted him. They had trusted the Logans, on their border ranch east of Nogales, for Frank Logan, sympathetic with a race which valued freedom so passionately, always made sure that small caches of food were left where the Indians could find them. And young Tom Logan, this second year after his father's death, had continued the custom.

Riding up through the timbered ridges of his Cerro Alto pasture, Logan came to a clearing. In the center of it was a rude corral of mesquite limbs—one of his line camps. He listened with pleasure to the cool and tinkling music of water dripping into a mossy cement trough beside the corral. He pulled a blue bandanna from his pocket and wiped the sweat from his face as he glanced around.

Much of the ground was shaded by a giant mesquite, as large as an eastern oak. He reined over to the tree and gazed up among its lower branches, then rose on the stirrups to pull a gunnysack from a nail driven into a branch. He shook the sack, and smiled. It was empty.

The Yaqui weather had started.

He swung down and untied a grain sack lashed behind his saddle. Tall and lightly built, blond and gray-eyed, he was twenty-two but looked much younger. He was completely serious about himself and his role as a rancher. Hard work and long days kept the fat off a rancher in this country—kept him from a lot of foolishness in fact. When his father died, after six months in bed, there was not enough money left to keep things going until the beef crop was made. So, still a minor by a year, Tom went into the Stockmen's Bank and asked to borrow nine hundred dollars.

Without a moment's hesitation, the banker gave it to him. 'What I like about you,' he told Tom, 'is that you don't confuse your wants with your necessities.'

Logan was young enough to be impressed. He took the banker's words both as praise and as a solemn charge to be faithful to the contract he had entered into. Six months later he was able to pay it off. He felt such a sense of achievement afterward that he considered borrowing again just for the satisfaction of paying off ahead of time.

Logan hung the grain sack from the limb where the other had hung. Though two-thirds empty, it contained sugar, *harina* for tortillas, and dried meat. Suddenly, as he made the sack secure, the breeze brought a rank odor to his nostrils. He wrinkled his nose. Back in the brush, squirming with maggots, he would find the rotting carcass of a calf he would never tally in the roundup.

While his horse drank at the trough, he gazed about the clearing. From a thicket came the woody notes of a cardinal. Cerro Alto was his poorest pasture, too rugged to make fat cattle; but he liked the area better than the dun-colored valley where the old ranch house was located. Once in a while, time permitting; he came here to hunt the cats that hunted his calves. But hunting was a luxury he could seldom afford. The practical way was to keep a

Mexican operating a trap-line part of the year.

The horse raised its dripping muzzle from the trough, looked about, and resumed drinking. Glancing at the sack in the tree, Logan closed one eye. Now, he reflected: Did Julio get that food, or did the Indians? The Mexican had been up here for a month, with a young nephew named Miguel helping him. Riding up, Logan had seen a few cats with ears cut off draped over tree branches. The ears were by way of tallying.

He glanced around before mounting. In a short time he would be branding cattle here. There was salt, and the corral was sound. But there was no wood beside the firering, and the shovel he kept here was missing. He frowned. It was out of character for the Yaquis to steal, or to neglect a detail like firewood for the next man. He shrugged and rode out.

Fifty yards down the trail, his horse snorted and took a jump sideways. 'Ho!' He curbed the horse, peering into the brush. Again he smelled the rank odor he had noted before. This time it was so strong that he almost gagged.

Then he noted a shallow scoop in the earth beside the trail.

It resembled a wild pig wallow, except that the ground was dry. He urged the horse across the trail and reined in above the hole. Something had died and had been buried here and dug up again—the stench and flies told him that. Hoof prints patterned the earth—too many for Julio and Miguel to have left. Yaquis? No. The Yaquis were foot soldiers, not horsemen. When they traveled, they walked.

He saw a flutter of red cloth in the brush, and reined closer to pull a neckerchief from a branch. It was the type that many Yaquis wore knotted about their throats. But it was very old and filthy, and all at once he realized that it, too, stank of rottenness. He dropped it and rubbed his hand on his pants. Finally he got down and inspected the hole. It was about eight feet long, its floor dark and greasy. Flies, rising in a humming swarm, began settling on his face and forearms. He backed off with an oath, brushing them away.

Worried, now, he thought of Julio.

The Yaquis would murder any Mexican they caught, but not on this side of the line. Here, they were on good behavior, desiring above all else to preserve their lifeline to Tucson.

He was not sure how Julio felt about Yaquis. From time to time he went back to Sonora to stay with relatives for a few weeks. Was he so full of atrocious stories that he would murder a Yaqui soldier if he thought he could get away with it? Logan did not believe it. Julio respected a bargain, and knew an unspoken bargain existed between the American ranchers and the Yaquis. *You ignore us; we ignore you.*

But a body had lain in this hole for a week or longer before it had been dug up. Animals had not dragged it out, for the grave had been carefully excavated along its entire length.

He rode on, his mouth set.

The trail followed a shallow canyon under a cliff stained red and green by minerals, and pocked with caves. One of the caves was the 'mailbox' where he occasionally left information for Yaqui eyes only: that a Mexican, possibly one of the government's secret *corps de vada*, had been asking questions about Yaquis in the area . . .

The trail crossed a small rock-slide and emerged into a small, sandy area bare of trees but edged with brush and rocks. Logan slowed down and looked the ground over as he advanced. He saw no flash of sun on harness, smelled no smoke. The sand was almost bare. Beside the trail, however, rested, two round black stones, looking like a symbol of some kind.

Suddenly, startled, he pulled up.

They were not stones. They were heads.

Resting neatly three feet apart on the sand, they faced west, their backs to him. 'My God!' he whispered. His stomach began to convulse, as though a string, anchored to the pit of it, were being given a series of small, playful twitches. The hair on the heads was black and dusty.

Trembling inside, he made a long, careful

examination of the cliffs and hillsides. At last, wiping his mouth on his sleeve, he rode toward the heads. As he did so, one of the heads began to topple over. Then he realized the head was merely turning—that the rest of the body was buried alive in the sand!

He could see the man's face, now, distorted with terror. It was Julio. Logan yelled a word of encouragement and spurred his horse.

The Mexican rocked his head back and forth. 'No, *patron*! Save yourself! *Indios! Indios!*'

Logan dropped the reins and jumped from the saddle. The horse set its hoofs and stopped. He landed on his heels and sprawled beside Julio. There were flies all over the man's face, and he brushed them off angrily. The boy, Miguel, was weeping hysterically. Logan patted his head, feeling the grotesqueness of the gesture, and grinned.

'You're all right, Miguelito,' he said. 'Hush up, or you'll bring them back—'

Julio was praying. *'Padre Nuestro que seas en el cielo—sanctificado sea Tu Nombre—'*

Beside Logan's knee the sand exploded, covering him with grit. He heard a bullet scream off across the wash, then the whip-lashing report of a rifle shot. He froze, afraid to turn. After the shot, and the echoes cascading down the canyon, he heard nothing. But he knew they were coming.

He had a fleeting wish that his father were

alive and with him. His father had known how to talk to them. All the younger Logan had was the recollection of sitting silently at camp fires while his father and two or three Yaquis smoked and talked.

This would be the palaver at which he did the talking. He had better say a lot of right things, he knew, or the show was over. Slowly he stood up, and now he heard them trotting almost soundlessly over the sand.

CHAPTER TWO

As he looked at the faces of the Yaquis, he realized he knew none of them. He knew Saturnino, the Yaqui general of the northern area, and he knew his sons, but he recognized none of the twelve or fifteen Yaqui soldiers surrounding them now.

All the Indians wore ordinary peasant trousers, wrinkled and grease-stained, and collarband shirts buttoned nearly to the neck with neckerchiefs knotted about their throats. Their faces were raisin-brown, and most of the men were nearly as tall as Logan. All but one wore low-crowned straw hats; this man wore a red headband ornamented with a few small seashells. All carried modern rifles. In addition, one man carried Logan's missing shovel.

Logan stared at the soldier who wore the headband. Middle-aged, shorter than the others, he had coarse gray hair cut in bangs across the brow, and a wispy Oriental mustache. In one hand he carried a flat Yaqui war drum.

'I'm Tom Logan. These *lloris* work for me,' Logan said. 'What have they done?'

'They have murdered two of the kin,' the older Yaqui said, in Spanish.

The kin. Yaqui talk for any member of a village. *Lloris* was the generic term for Mexicans: crybabies. Logan looked at Julio.

'Did you do it?' he asked.

Julio started to babble denial, but the Yaqui with the headband struck a handful of sand in his face. '*Llori!*' he spat. 'All the same! They kill two of my soldiers. They rob them.'

Logan's mouth was dry as plaster. He tried to work up spit. A good way to convince an Indian you were telling the truth, his father used to tell him, is to spit. Indians knew a scared man's mouth was dry. He bit his tongue hard and a little saliva came.

He spat. It made a satisfactory sound on the sand.

'They didn't kill anybody,' he said. 'They may be *lloris*, but they're honest. I wouldn't hire anybody who wasn't honest. Where's Saturnino?'

The Indian raised his little war drum and thumped it. From the trees somewhere out of sight another drum thudded in response. Then horses moved on the shale.

'Saturnino is in Sonora,' the Yaqui said. 'The kin call me Pistola. Do you own this land?'

'Yes, sir. You bet. I'm Frank Logan's son. Saturnino used to call me Tomasito, when he'd stop for a smoke with my father.'

Pistola turned his head. '*Caita tiempo!*' he cried, in Yaqui, and the horses came faster. Logan twisted to watch them come. Two soldiers were leading a pair of pack animals across the wash, while two followed, switching at their legs. Someone took his revolver. The soldiers around him fell back to make room for the horses. The animals were halted and the men pulled back part of the tarpaulins over their loads . . .

There was a nightmarish moment of death settling like grease on his tongue, of his stomach squeezing as he looked at a head half-stripped of flesh and crawling with maggots. Julio was wailing his innocence in two languages.

Logan merely concentrated on not getting sick.

He heard a shovel grating in the sand, and blinked at the hole a warrior was digging.

'Chief, you're making a mistake,' he said calmly, but with the beat of his pulse in his throat. 'I'm the kin's friend. I leave food for you—'

Pistola touched his forehead and bowed his head. '*Muchas gracias.* How much it cost? Ten pesos? All right. Now you steal two saddlebags of gold!'

He shoved out his hand, opening it in an angry gesture-like spitting. Five golden coins lay in his palm. They were all of the same size, and were foreign. The shovel was still scraping at the sand. Pistola dropped a coin in Logan's shirt pocket.

'A man should not die with empty pockets,' he said.

'Do you think I killed your men?' Logan asked gravely.

'We found the pack horses near your camp. The coyotes had already found the men. The coins were in the brush near the saddlebags.'

When it was finished, the hole was about three feet deep. Logan was ordered to sit down in it, cross-legged. Then one of the soldiers began to fill it with sand. He had his choice, now, of being buried to the neck like the others, for whatever torture came after, or of committing suicide by trying to escape.

He sat down. Though quick death would be preferable to a slow one; he banked on his knowledge of the Indians. Pistola derided the help he had given 'the kin.' But honor was a sort of sickness with the Yaqui. He was not cured of it in a moment of anger.

The boy, Miguel, had ceased to cry, while Julio borrowed stoicism from Logan's behavior and ceased to beg and argue with the soldiers.

'The horses,' said the chief.

Three of his men mounted the captured ponies. They were not horsemen, and Logan's already nervous animal wheeled and offered trouble. There was no steel at the heels of the young soldier who rode him, but he was finally controlled. At last, the three horses were lined up a hundred feet down the wash, facing the heads grotesquely lined up on the sand.

'Close your eyes,' Logan murmured, in Spanish.

The drum uttered its hard, unresonant sound and the horses raced forward. His eyes shut, he bit his lip as they came. He heard and felt their thunder in his body, then grit stung his face. Wind whipped his hair as a horse jumped him. Miguel cried out. The hoofs were behind them, then, halting a few rods beyond.

In a moment the horses ran back.

Pistola played this game for fifteen minutes. Logan's eyes, ears, and hair were filled with sand.

At last it ended. They dug him from the sand but left the Mexicans buried.

'Where is the gold?' asked Pistola.

Logan raised his shoulders. 'How much am I supposed to have stolen? If I have enough, I will pay it to save my people.'

'Do you have ten thousand dollars?' asked Pistola.

Logan halted in the act of working sand from his shirt. 'Ten thousand!'

'In Spanish gold,' said the Yaqui. 'The dead men you saw were taking it to Tucson to buy supplies.'

There were legends of buried treasure in the mountains of Sonora. The Jesuits were supposed to have buried the gold in the mission cemeteries when the King of Spain ordered them home, replacing them with monks of the Franciscan order.

'I've got a few hundred dollars in the bank,' Tom Logan said.

With stony eyes, the chief retorted: 'You will bring the money to the cave within two weeks, or the *lloris* will pay your debt. And not only they. If the American ranchers are no longer our friends, then they are enemies. If they are enemies, they will find it safer to move into Nogales.'

Logan knelt to gaze into Julio's sad, frightened features. 'Did you do it, Julio?'

'*Patrón*, by the most Holy Mary—!'

Logan ruffled his hair. 'All right. I'll get the money somehow. They won't hurt you for two weeks, and that will give me time to scratch it up.'

Ten thousand to raise on a six-thousand-dollar ranch? He sighed. Well, maybe. Rising stiffly, he pulled off his shirt as the Yaqui soldiers watched.

'There are other ranchers,' he argued.

'There's a woman near my place named Laura Sutton who has a new foreman. And there's a man named Barksdale.'

'Barksdale does not ranch in the mountains,' the chief remarked.

'He might ride to the mountains, though.'

'I will talk to Barksdale,' said Pistola.

'Do you know him?' Logan asked, surprised.

Ignoring the question, Pistola turned his back. He ordered the extra horses unsaddled and turned loose. He uttered another order and men began digging sand away from the buried men. Then he turned back.

'When you wish to see me, build a fire before the cave.'

Logan finished working the sand from his clothes and underwear, while the soldiers tied the prisoner's hands behind their backs, using hobbles from their own gear to chain them together by their ankles before prodding them toward the hillside. Pistola and two soldiers remained with Logan.

The chief told him, 'I release you because if you have the money, it may be you will bring it back. If I kill you now, the money too is dead. If you bring the money back, I will let you leave safely. But if you do not come back with the money, I give you my word ranches will burn, and men and cattle will die. This has not happened before, and it will not happen again. *Palabra de inglés!*'

*   *   *

Logan rode away.

Palabra de inglés: 'Word of an Englishman,' the strongest oath they could take. Strange people. Somewhere, back in their history, they had had dealings with an Englishman, probably a miner who had dealt honestly with them. They hated Spaniards and Mexicans, had also slaughtered the mission fathers from time to time, yet they worshiped the Spanish God—or the pagan deity they imagined to be his god.

And until a day or two ago they had classed Americans as honest and dependable.

Reaching the line camp, Logan scrubbed his forehead on his sleeve and thought grimly. Two weeks! To find a cache of Spanish gold buried in the mountains—or in a desert arroyo—or on a train rattling across the country. He pulled the saddle off the horse and turned the animal into the corral while he nosed around.

He sat on the edge of the water trough, his eyes roving the camp. He pictured the soldiers reaching the spot and turning the animals into the corral. Men who had walked thirty miles today, but were not tired. Lifting off the heavy packs, then dragging down the sack to see what Tomasito, son of old Don Pancho, had left them. Sitting down to chew on dried antelope meat, mixing a gruel of *panola*, maybe some wild honey in water for a drink. Then the shots. Stinging out of the brush a second ahead of the thunder, killing them instantly.

He chewed his lip. *Had* to be more than one man. One man couldn't handle two Yaquis even with a headstart. Julio had a single-shot Ballard and no pistol. Suppose, because they trusted him as an *empleado* of Tomasito, they let him come up and talk to them. Then, suddenly, Julio swung the rifle up.

He shook his head. The Mexican would have been knocked out of his boots the first time he even *looked* at that rifle, let alone pulled it from the boot. They didn't trust any *llori* that far.

So it had to be from ambush. But the Yaquis invented ambush. To walk into a trap—two of the big war chief's picked soldiers, carrying a fortune—was beyond belief.

The horse was wriggling on its back, covering itself with straw and dirt. Logan put his hands on his knees and scowled. Why had the men been buried in that particular spot, fifty yards down the trail? Perhaps because the earth was looser and made easier digging. But why bury the men at all?

He broke a piece of mesquite to the length of a cane and poked around in the brush, looking for cartridges or loose coins. Why, he wondered, had there been any loose coins at all?

Another thing that puzzled him was how anyone had known that the soldiers were coming, or, seeing the pack horses, had divined that they were laden with more than Indian grub, turkey feathers, and masks for a celebration on their Sunday off.

After an hour, he gave up and rubbed the horse down with a gunny sack. He had found nothing. There was only one answer: the thieves had known the Yaquis personally. They had known the Yaquis were coming. Having used this leverage to murder them, they had sprinkled a few coins around, buried the bodies just under the surface of the earth, and thus made sure the next group of Indians to come through would discover the crime and go looking for the man on whose land the atrocity had been committed. The only kind of man who could kill the Indians so easily was another Indian. And if that was what had happened, he could search the rest of his life and never find him.

Or suppose it was another rancher, someone they trusted.

Barksdale? He was new here, had been a freighter before buying the run-down old Hamilton place a year ago. Or Laura Sutton, who was busy buying handsome, worthless horseflesh to pull her buggies while she ran her ranch into the ground. Hardly.

But her foreman, now—the shiftless

Breen—*there* was a possibility.

He got up wearily and entered the corral. Tomorrow he'd talk to Barksdale, then ride over to the Sutton ranch and talk to her and Breen. And meantime get out the old family Bible his father had read so much the last few months of his life, and try to find some comfort in it.

CHAPTER THREE

An hour before sunset, Clyde Barksdale sauntered onto the gallery of his ranch house with a bottle of Mexican *aguardiente* and a pottery cup. He wore black linsey-woolsey pants but no shirt; his barrel chest was covered with gray underwear buttoned to the throat. He was a roughly-made man whose frame was timbered with thick muscles and wide bones. His features were dark and leathery, deeply creased from staring the sun down on a dozen deserts. Under a strong brow, his eyes were keen and black.

Barksdale dropped into a leather chair, propped his feet on the rail, and pulled the cork from the bottle with his teeth. He poured two inches of brandy, drank off half of it, and sighed. Then he tilted his head against the raw adobe wall; feeling the prickle of the straw the Mexicans stirred into the mud when they trampled up a batch of bricks. He had built the house—shoebox shaped, with a tin roof and a jacklegged gallery—when he bought this ranch a year ago. A slope staked with small, brittle trees climbed from his back door to a level rimrock plateau a hundred feet above. The whole layout was very plain. In addition to the house, there were a corral, a shelter for dry feed, and a lean-to where his Mexican couple lived. He had not wanted to sink much money in the place, because he expected presently to move to better quarters. But it suited him for the moment, and so did the valley on the north slope of which it lay, shallow and dun-colored in winter; green, now, and silvered with cottonwoods along the watercourses.

Barksdale finished the brandy, his eyes watering as it seared his gullet, and poured another drink. He liked to sit and watch the day bleed into night. A rosy light from the hills to the west flooded his valley so that the rough little hillocks on the floor of it floated like islands.

One thing prevented his full enjoyment of the scene: he actually owned only a little wedge of that valley. The eastern end of it, smothered in haze, belonged to the coming-yearlin' named Tom Logan—the rest, running west to the Santa Cruz River, was the property of Laura Sutton.

He meant to own all of that valley, and a chunk more besides. He was new to ranching, and not doing too almighty well, but he was learning. And it beat freighting by a bucketful. Twenty years he had had of that trade, hauling down from El Paso and Tucson into Mexico.

That hot Sonoran desert! Two months from now, beyond the mountains, the sun would curl your eyelashes. Once he had, as a companion, a professor of medicine who wanted to study the effects of heat prostration. Barksdale had felt fortunate to get him out alive, brain-baked and corroded with dysentery. No better place in the world to study heat prostration.

Suddenly the big man leaned forward. Out there in the dusk of the valley something had moved.

His black eyes glittered with interest. It had not been cattle, or he'd have seen horns flash. A horse would have stood out clearly, too. Barksdale stepped into the cabin and emerged with a folding German spyglass. Going to one knee, he rested his elbows on the railing and peered through the glass, screwing the eyepiece to sharpen the focus.

After a moment he lowered the glass and thoughtfully collapsed it. He chewed his lip and pondered, then turned his head to call toward the shack where his Mexicans lived.

'Oye, Chaparro!'

The little handyman came almost at a run. Smiling, mustached, looking like a miniature cavalry general disguised as a civilian,

Chaparro touched his fingertips to his brow.

'Mánde?'

'Saddle me a horse,' Barksdale said.

'Will you not eat dinner, *patrón*?'

'No. *Aprisa!*'

Barksdale jogged down the long slope of the valley toward a dry wash a mile away. Behind the saddle he carried some provisions rolled in an oilskin. Once, from high ground, he observed a gleam of light on the far slope of the valley: Laura Sutton's place. Sleep on the roof for a couple of weeks, Missy! thought Barksdale. A tenderfoot like you wouldn't cotton to Yaqui weather even in normal times.

And it ain't going to be normal for a while.

After a twenty-minute ride, with darkness beginning to enfold the valley, he came to a ruined ranch house on the bank of a wash. Two walls remained standing in a broken angle, the wind hissed through apertures and the brittle framework of fruit trees in a family orchard. After tying the horse, Barksdale carried the oilskin roll toward the adobe walls, still unmelted by the summer rains. Humming to himself, he stepped into the enclosed corner.

He pulled up short. Three men squatted in the shelter of the walls. He stared at them as the men rose in silence.

'Hey—what the hell!' he growled, stepping back.

A man responded in the Yaqui dialect. 'The

kin salute you.'

Barksdale chuckled and stepped forward, touching his hat brim in respect to the rank of the man whose voice he recognized. The Indian returned his salute, and they gripped hands. Then the four squatted down and Barksdale rolled a cigarette for each of them,

'How's the war going?' he asked.

General Luis Muñoz—who called himself Pistola in this country—explained that Chief Cajeme, leader of all the Eight Pueblos, had recently destroyed the remnants of Topete's Mexican army—the second army the Yaquis had fatally mauled in three years. But other soldiers were coming in, and peons were being conscripted in the villages. The action might come earlier next fall, though summer heat would enforce the usual lull.

'And how is the life of a rancher?' asked Pistola, politely.

'Oh, hell—there ain't no easy way to make a dollar,' said Barksdale. 'I've got to spread out or starve.'

'Freighting for the kin was easy,' said Pistola.

'Wouldn't 've been if I'd got caught,' Barksdale said.

He had practically kept the war going single-handedly for years, with the munitions and critical supplies he had freighted in. How he used to dread those rendezvous in the foothills! Unloading wagons to throw out valuable cargo underneath, then repacking before daylight. With Porfirio's Goddamn Dorado circulating around all over Sonora—tougher, prettier, and smarter than any Texas Ranger he'd ever butted his head against. Woodsmen, gunmen, trackers—all in one skinny-legged red and gray uniform.

'But you never *got* caught,' the general reminded him. 'Was the pay not good enough?'

'You bet I never got caught—wouldn't be here if I had. Sure, the pay was fine, General. But Jesus, a man's luck don't last forever . . .'

'No,' the general agreed stolidly. Then he told of the murder of his soldiers, who were traveling to Tucson with over ten thousand dollars in gold.

* * *

Barksdale was surprised and shocked.

They discussed how it might have happened. Pistola asked questions about the ranchers in the area.

'Do you know the man who ranches east of you?' he asked.

'Sure—feller named Tom Logan. I don't know him very well. I offered to buy his land when I settled here, but I couldn't get it so I bought this other little spread. But if you want to hear Logan knocked,' he grinned, 'talk to my neighbor on the west—Laura Sutton.'

'A woman?'

'*All* woman. From Pennsylvania, or somewheres back there. She wouldn't give Logan the sleeves out of her vest—if she wore one.'

'Why?'

The spark of Barksdale's wheat-straw cigarette traced a wave of his hand. 'Well, she's got this crazy female notion that Logan killed her brother,' he drawled.

He drew on the cigarette, knowing he was on trial. He knew these people too well to be fooled. It must be in Pistola's mind that those men of his—picked, trained, devoted—could not possibly have failed him by blundering into an ambush. So maybe they had been murdered by friends . . .

'Probably just a female notion,' the freighter repeated. 'The woman and her brother came to Arizona three years ago and bought this ranch. I gather they inherited some money in the East. But Alden Sutton was a booze fighter, and the idea was that he'd dry out on a ranch and make a man of himself. He was no damn shakes of a rancher, though, and everybody hoorawed him and took advantage of him. When he bought a ton of hay it was half rocks. Logan whipped his ass in a poker game at Nacho Ruiz's saloon one night and won all his cash. Sutton started home. In the morning they found him and his horse in a wash. He'd rode the critter right off a thirty-foot cutbank.'

He shrugged: 'Anyway, that's what the Sutton woman tells me, and what I pick up in town. He was probably drunk. But I reckon Logan pretty nigh wrecked him that night.'

The Indians smoked silently, holding the butts awkwardly, like men who had never smoked before. They had their own little smokes, called *hiak bibas*—small and potent as firecrackers—and they were smoking his Bull Durham to be polite. A coyote chorus howled in the distance. The breeze blew steady.

'Money like that don't keep quiet long, General,' Barksdale reflected. 'Sooner or later, it'll work to the surface. When do you figure they were killed?'

'Two weeks past.'

Barksdale frowned at the tip of his cigarette. 'Two weeks—' he reflected. 'What's been goin' on in the last two weeks? Logan's Mexican's been trapping puma in his mountain range. My men—I've only got two—have been getting things ready for the calf count. A peddler with a wagon was through one day, but I think he headed on up the valley to Tucson. Joe Breen's been out of town for two weeks—'

'Who is Breen?' asked Pistola.

'Miss Sutton's ramrod. I found him for her after her brother died. Hard-nosed bastard, but I figured that was what she needed. Breen went over to Bisbee, on business. Reckon he's due back about tomorrow.'

He sensed that the Yaqui was dissatisfied, and knew that the chief, for all the friendship that had bound them, might be thinking: And what have *you* been doing for the last two weeks, my friend?

'Like I say,' Barksdale said, 'that kind of mercy don't rest easy. Whoever's got it will start spending it. If it was a rancher, he'll buy him a registered bull, or build his wife a couple of new rooms—something like that. Was this paper money or gold?'

'Spanish gold.'

Barksdale took the cigarette to his lips, drew on it, and dropped it. 'Good. Where can he spend it that it won't set people talking? And when they talk, General, I'll be listening.'

Pistola rose from the floor. 'I hope it will be soon, friend. I cannot go back to Chief Cajeme until I recover the money, or exact payment. In two weeks, the kin who are already working in Arizona will be ordered back.'

Barksdale rose beside him. 'I hope your soldiers will know old friends from *llori* lovers,' he said pointedly.

'After two weeks,' Pistola said sharply, 'we will have no friends.'

* * *

When the Yaquis had trotted silently down the wash, Barksdale leaned against a wall and listened to the night sounds. He exhaled his breath. Man!

A couple of miles away he saw Laura Sutton's lights. He'd have to warn her to move into town. He could drive the best of her cattle—which wasn't saying much—up onto his land where they'd be safe from the Indians. For in spite of Pistola's threat to raid friends and enemies alike, he knew the general would not carry it out. It was a curious fact, that the less a people had, the more value they placed on honor and friendship.

* * *

In the morning, Barksdale did some ciphering.

His troubles weren't all spelled *Yaqui*. For his cash was running low, and the prospects he worked out on paper left him frowning. So many calves to sell next fall, at so much a head. Hell of it was, the buyers paid so little for feeders. It was all killers, two-year-olds or better. That meant that during a man's first two years in the beef business, nothing was coming in.

On top of that, he'd been sold a lot of worthless mother-stuff for his calve-stocked herd, cows that had already had the last calves they were going to have in this world. And a bull he'd paid five hundred dollars for seemed inclined like that young fellow in the big saloon in Hermosillo, that they called Maria Elena—the damned bull trailed around after the steers and left the cows alone. He'd tried block and tackle even, but it was no go.

Alden Sutton, the boozing easterner, wasn't the only man who'd been made an ass of.

But Sutton's way out was to kill himself. Barksdale's way was going to be direct action.

* * *

The Sutton girl, now. Shaving on the gallery in midafternoon, Barksdale peered across the valley at the haze of trees that marked the Sutton ranch. He decided he had let far too much time pass before pressing her. He'd helped Laura in many ways. Had found her a foreman who—for all his ineptitude with cattle—had put an end to such nonsense as merchants selling her weevilly grain and short-weight hay. Joe Breen had left a trail of skinned noses and scared merchants around Nogales.

Now it was time to let her know the season was changing.

In this country, a woman needed a man. But sometimes she needed to be reminded of it. Barksdale couldn't think of a better time to remind Laura than tonight.

He dressed in the style of a rich Mexican rancher, the garb he had found it politic to wear in Mexico and now felt comfortable in: black trousers, a small-lapelled coat, and a cone-peaked sombrero. He buckled on a Colt with silver grips, mounted his horse, and swung by the Mexican's shack.

'Anybody asks,' he told Chaparro, 'I'm going for a little *pasear*. Keep the damn chickens off the porch. I'll be back late.'

'Bien, patrón. Que te vaya bien!'

Barksdale rode away, square-shouldered and easy in the saddle.

When he had ridden a mile, he saw a horseman off to the southeast, heading toward his ranch. Barksdale immediately dropped into a small arroyo, and kept riding south, He preferred to put off the meeting with Tom Logan for a while.

He reckoned where Hatcher and Price, his cowhands, would be about now, and took a line toward his Alamo Prieto pasture, where they were supposed to be building a corral for use during the calf-cut.

The men were there, all right. Barksdale peered at the pair from a hundred yards off—sitting on the ground having a smoke by their cook-fire—at five o'clock! He scowled and shook his head. Both men had been with him when he had his freight string; good, steady hands who didn't fly apart under fire. But Goddamn! they were as lazy as two steers in a feed lot, without somebody to ramrod them.

The men were working hard when he entered the camp. Hatcher, a very tall man with curly blond hair and baked red skin, was at it with a posthole digger. Price, a wiry man with a chipmunk face, was swinging an axe against a mesquite pole. Only one thing was right about the picture: their rifles lay within arm's reach of where they worked.

Hatcher looked up as Barksdale reined in beside him. He pulled out a bandanna to wipe his brow. 'Evening, Clyde,' he said.

Barksdale muttered a greeting. He counted the posts they had erected, then gazed at the campfire.

'Something smells good,' he said ironically. 'You men already ate supper?'

Price made a gesture. 'Lemme give you a bait of stew,' he said heartily. 'Hatch and I usually eat about this time and then work till dark . . .'

'You mean you knock off about three and *eat* till dark, don't you?' Barksdale said, sourly. 'How long did it take you to stick those posts in the ground?'

Hatcher's long frame shook as he jarred the posthole digger into the stony earth. 'Best part of the day,' he admitted. 'But hear all the rocks in this ground!'

'Throw that damned posthole digger away and use a shovel,' Barksdale growled. 'There's no easy way to dig in Arizona. If you men are too stupid to learn a new trade, just say so. I'll give you a letter to Southwest Cartage and you can climb back onto a wagon.'

Price's long face, with his heavy eyelids and full cheeks, looked injured. 'You don't toughen up to a new trade overnight, Clyde,' he said.

'You damn well better,' Barksdale retorted. 'Overnight is how I cut into ranching, and overnight is how I'll go broke if I don't cut it this year. You savvy?'

'You bet,' Hatcher said, reaching for the shovel.

'Let it go,' Barksdale told him. 'We're riding over to Miss Sutton's tonight.'

While they saddled, he shoveled dirt onto the campfire. 'Watch out for yourselves from now on,' he said. 'The Yaquis are on the prowl. General Muñoz paid me a call last night. Somebody killed a couple of his men on Logan's range.'

Hatcher whistled. 'Mexican patrol, you reckon? That'd be one for the army, wouldn't it?'

'I don't know. But in case he shoves a gun in your mouth and asks where you were two weeks ago, tell him the truth: you were building a dirt dam for me on Deer Creek.'

The men nodded. Like Barksdale, they knew the Yaqui temperament and were not unduly disturbed.

'And if he asks where *I* was, just say I was with you. I was in Tucson buying that windmill, if you remember, but it'd be simpler not to have to get affidavits to prove it—with a skinning knife stuck in my throat.'

A half hour before dark, they reached the Sutton ranch, a comfortable sprawl of buildings on a hillside at the mouth of a creek. Big trees in new leaf would cast ample shade when the heat came. The main building had a whitewashed stone foundation and adobe walls, with a comfortable gallery partly screened by honeysuckle. The place was old and solid. Barksdale pulled in his horse and wiped dust from his face with a handkerchief.

'Tom Logan may come around,' he said. 'I'm going to be busy with the lady of the house, so just tell him there's nobody home.'

'Who're me and Price gonna be busy with?' Hatcher asked.

Barksdale chuckled. 'I'll send the cook out to entertain you.'

From the pocket of his coat, he pulled a flat bottle of tequila, oily and yellow, and tossed it to the men.

'Go easy on this stuff,' he said, 'I've heard drinking it will grow hair on the palms of your hands.'

Then he reset his big hat and rode into the ranch yard.

CHAPTER FOUR

Barksdale's Mexican could tell Tom Logan nothing he did not already know. Chaparro had insisted that he come into the *jacál* he occupied with his wife. The little woman, swarthy with Indian blood, her black hair hanging in braids, stood aside while they sat at the table and talked. The shack was dirt-floored, but everything was spotless. Chaparro was as proud of his home as any Sonoran *hacendado*.

But he had seen no Yaquis recently—no strange gringos—no Mexican soldiers. Was there something wrong? he asked.

'Plenty wrong,' Logan told him. 'You'd better mark the fifteenth on your calendar, and unless I send word to you, move into town then.'

* * *

As he explained about the murders, Chaparro's wife began to wail. She knew all about Yaquis. She was ready to move into Nogales tonight.

'There's no danger right now,' Logan said. 'They don't want trouble any more than we do—probably less. Do you like working for Barksdale?' he asked Chaparro.

'*Asi, asi*,' shrugged the Mexican. 'It's a job, eh?'

'Tell you how you can make fifty dollars American right quick,' Logan said. If you see anything suspicious, ride over and tell me about it. Any strangers—any Dorados—any digging.'

'*Si, patrón. Que mal haya!*'

Logan rose from the table and offered his hand and a smile. 'Don't worry. Let the guilty ones worry.'

The valley was dark when Logan reached Laura Sutton's ranch. The home place was exceptionally well-situated, only a half mile from the county road on high ground. It had made a good living for old man Lincoln, the previous owner, but Sutton money had put a curse on it. No wonder! For all Alden Sutton knew about beef was that it made good steak; and his sister knew even less. And now, with a foreman like Joe Breen, the ranch was in delicate health indeed.

The yard was big and dark. He made out the pitiful skeletons of the rose bushes Laura Sutton had set out, and her tulip trees, planted from bare-root stock, which had withered in a few months. Easterners and their plants rooted poorly in the brick-oven soil of the border country.

Looking for a place to tie his horse—the rack had come down to make room for the rose bushes—he rode toward the corral. The horse quivered suddenly and stopped. He took it in hand, staring into the darkness. Two men rose from the ground in his path.

'Hello!' he said.

'Howdy Mr. Logan,' a man said. Logan saw the glint of a rifle, and he felt a lash of anger.

'Hatcher?' he said.

'That is correct. Reckon you can find your

way back, Mr. Logan.'

'What's the game?' Logan asked.

'No game. They're talking business in the house, and the word was they don't want to be tormented by guests.'

*   *   *

Looking for Barksdale had been a good hunch, Logan decided. He wondered how acute these men of his were. He could smell tequila on the tall, red-faced one standing nearest him, so perhaps they weren't at their best.

He started to swing from the saddle, but saw both men press forward. Leaning on the swell of the saddle, then, he loosened the thong which held his catch-rope.

'What's going on?' he asked.

The smaller man, the offscrapings called Price, moved closer to Hatcher. 'Nobody ever tells us anything,' he said. 'Did you want to see the boss lady, or Clyde?'

'Both.'

'Come back tomorrow,' Hatcher said.

'You damned fools,' Logan snapped. 'I came to talk to Laura Sutton. If she doesn't want to see me, get one of her people to tell me so.'

Carefully, he lifted the coil of manila from the saddle and started sliding rope through the honda with his thumb.

'I'll say it once more,' Hatcher told him.

'Miz Sutton don't want to see you. Clyde don't want to see you. The only way you're going is out. Now, git."

'I don't give a damn whether she wants to talk to me or not. It's as important to her as it is to me. That goes for your boss, too.'

'Why don't you write it down,' Price suggested, 'and we'll have the maid take it inside?'

'Go to hell,' Logan snapped. 'Tell them I was here.'

He swung the horse, rode a few feet, and twisted in the saddle. As he did so, he hurled the rope. The men heard it whistle and stepped back, confused as to what had made the sound. As the big noose settled over them, Logan threw a dally around the horn and spurred the pony. From the solid shock that traveled up the manila, he knew he had roped both of them. A gun hit the ground with a clank. Both men were swearing; then the sounds changed to yelps of pain as the horse dragged them over the ground. He kept the horse at a fast walk across the yard and up the wagon road, while the men howled their fury and pain. When the road dipped into a ravine, he turned the horse and rode down it. The shouting behind him ceased. Reining in, he listened. One of the men was moaning. He drew his Colt and rode back, jumped down, and made sure the fight was out of them. He checked them for weapons. There was still a

Colt in Hatcher's holster. He threw it aside. Finally he pulled the rope off them, coiled it, and remounted.

When he reached the ranch yard, two figures were silhouetted on the porch of the big ranch house—the smaller, a full-skirted feminine shape; the larger, the muscular, top-heavy outline of a very large man. Logan walked toward them between the lines of rose bushes.

'. . . Hatcher?' Clyde Barksdale called uneasily.

'Yeah, boss,' Tom Logan said, with mockery.

'What's all the—*Who is it*?' Barksdale cried, moving quickly to a place where he was not silhouetted against a window.

Logan stopped, his hand near his gun. 'It's Tom Logan. I've got some news for Miss Sutton.'

The girl replied in a haughty, modulated voice. 'I don't need news from you, Mr. Logan. All the news you've ever brought me has been bad. Please leave at once.'

'It's not a social call,' Logan said. 'If that makes any difference.'

The girl uttered a short laugh. 'Well, I certainly wouldn't think of doing *business* with you, Mr. Logan.'

Barksdale chuckled and came to the top of the steps. 'That's it, friend,' he said. 'When a lady makes up her mind, never try to change it.

Better go home and write her a letter.'

Logan kept his face turned toward the girl. Though she stood partly in shadow, he could see her clearly—her hair dark brown, her skin creamy, her nose small and fine. Her eyes were a strange, light gray, somehow compelling. A very pretty young woman and an unbelievably foolish one.

Logan pushed his hat back. 'I've just changed a couple of other people's minds,' he told him, 'so maybe I'll keep trying. Miss Sutton, do you ever worry about Indians?'

'No,' the girl replied, 'I'm not worried about Indians, witches, or spells. Do you think I should be?'

He nodded. 'I think you're going to be murdered, if you don't move into town.'

She laughed. 'If that's all you came for—to try to frighten me into selling my ranch, I suppose—I think it's in *very* bad taste.'

To Logan's surprise, Barksdale cleared his throat and said, with reluctance: 'He may be right, Miss Laura. That's one reason I rode down tonight—to warn you. I told a couple of my men to stop anybody that tried to ride up to the house, in case it was a war party.'

'That's not what they told me,' Logan said, drily.

'I don't care what they told you,' Barksdale retorted. 'That's what I told them.'

'. . . What is it?' Laura Sutton asked. 'Apaches—?'

Logan shook his head. 'Wish that was all. It's Yaquis. The Apaches raided into the Yaqui country once, but they never went again. And if the Yaquis come, this country will never forget it.'

Laura looked at him, then at Barksdale. At last she turned toward the door: 'Come in.'

*　　*　　*

They had been eating at a large table of golden oak. The dining room was long, with low ceilings, and was dimly lit by wall lamps. The floor was dark and oiled, with hide rugs over it. The girl called to a maid in broken Spanish before taking her place at the table. Barksdale resumed a seat before a cup of coffee.

Laura indicated by a gesture that Logan was to sit down. He did, as a Mexican girl brought coffee.

'What have *you* heard?' Logan asked Barksdale.

Barksdale rested his weight on the table by his elbows, his big, somnolent face dark. 'I heard that a couple of Yaqui dog soldiers were killed on your land,' he said.

'Where'd you hear this?'

'I got to know a few people in Sonora while I was in the freight trade. One of them came to me last night. How about you? Where'd you hear it?'

Logan told them about Pistola, and of his panther trapper, Julio. 'I've got two weeks, less a day,' he said, 'to find that money.'

Barksdale sucked a tooth. ' 'Pears to me the chief's going about things backwards. He oughtta torture the greaseballs first and find out where they hid the money.'

'Would they have stayed up there, if they'd done it?' Logan snapped. When Barksdale shrugged, he looked at the girl. 'Where's your foreman, Miss Laura?'

'I resent your implication.' Laura's chin went up.

'Resent, hell! We're in trouble. The only way we're going to save our necks is to leave the country or find the men who killed the soldiers. Where's Joe Breen?'

Laura glanced at Barksdale. Apparently he indicated that she should answer, for she brushed a wisp of hair from her brow and said: 'Joe's in Bisbee, on business.'

'Spring's a peculiar time to be away on business,' Logan commented. 'But then Breen's a peculiar foreman any way you figure it.'

Laura, kinking her fingers, gave him a little smile. 'And *just* what does that mean?'

'I mean that if I wanted to go broke the quickest way, Breen's the kind of short-pod hell-raiser I'd pick for a ramrod. He's bone lazy, can't judge cattle, and treats land like it was a rug he could replace when he'd worn it out.'

The girl was answering before he had finished. 'Joe's the best foreman in the county! Before he came, people were cheating me on everything I bought. Neighbors were letting their cattle stray over my range. He put a stop to those things in a hurry.'

Logan grinned. 'So now only Breen's taking advantage of you. At least you know who to blame.'

She crossed her arms. She was a fine-looking girl, he thought. Under normal circumstances he'd have been neglecting his work to pay court to her. A really beautiful woman—but hopelessly ignorant and set on a wrong path.

'Since the day we came here,' Laura said, 'you've made things as difficult for us as you could. I suppose it's the old story of the native resenting the outlander. Or it might go deeper, mightn't it? It might involve plans to buy my land when I finally give up—'

Logan looked down. It had crossed his mind, that after the Suttons had had enough, he might try to scratch up a down payment on the ranch in bankruptcy court.

He sipped his coffee. 'If it's up for grabs some day,' he said, 'I'll probably bid on it. Assuming I'm still alive. But I've never bucked you people, and I treated your brother like I'd treat anybody else, under the circumstances . . .'

'Under what circumstances?'

'I only talked to Alden a half-dozen times. And it usually started with him being on the prod about something. Once he said he'd seen me running his cattle. The truth was I found 'em in my priming pasture, hogging down all that good grass I'd been saving. So I chased 'em out.'

'There's chasing, and chasing,' Barksdale remarked. 'I heard you ran them so hard one of the cows broke a leg.'

'You heard wrong,' Logan said. 'When Alden was drinking, he'd say just about anything that came into his head. Maybe he lost a cow that week and decided to blame it on me. I don't know. Guess I didn't handle the man right. We tangled every time we met. But I've never been much good with drunks.' Then he bit his tongue, ashamed he had gone so far. He thought of apologizing.

It was too late. The girl's fists clenched and she leaned toward him. 'Now that he's gone, you can call him anything you want, can't you? His sister can't give you much trouble. But if I ever get a chance, Mr. Logan, I promise you'll be sorry for sending him to his death that night—'

Logan wagged his head, sighing. 'Miss Laura, there was a poker game at Nacho Ruiz's that night. Sometimes I take twenty dollars and take a hand in a card game—maybe twice a year. It's about my only recreation. Usually I lose. Is it sinful when I win, just because your brother was playing?'

'I don't mean that! I mean the way you humiliated and taunted him—kept him betting over his head—and sent him home desperate, knowing he'd gambled away fifty of our calves! The ones we were going to keep for the mother herd!'

Logan gazed helplessly at Barksdale. 'You were there, Barksdale. Back me up. I've never crowded a man in my life. Damn it, he crowded me! I couldn't afford stakes like that. But he kept jabbing at me—"Give me a chance to get even! Sky's the limit. Double or nothing." I was ready to quit at eleven.'

Laura's eyes beseeched Barksdale. 'Clyde, you said—'

The freighter's dark face brooded. He frowned, recollecting the night of Alden Sutton's death. 'All I remember—I heard somebody say, "Double or nothing! Let's end this." I looked around, and there was only the two of you at the table and you were shaking your finger under his nose and yelling at him. Sutton got a pencil out of his pocket and wrote something on the back of a dollar bill.'

Laura smiled stiffly. 'I still have the dollar bill. What he wrote was, "Give bearer fifty calves on demand." I paid Mr. Logan two hundred dollars for that bill after the funeral.'

'How much were the calves worth?' Logan demanded. 'Five hundred? Six hundred? To cover eight hundred dollars cash I had on the table.'

Barksdale laughed. 'Being's you only started with twenty, boy, I'd say you weren't risking a lot.'

Both of them looked at him as though he had been found out in something shameful, the girl's eyes flashing in bitter triumph. Logan pushed his coffee away and stood up.

'We're not getting far,' he said. 'I'm sorry about all of it. But there's nothing anybody can do now. All I'm saying is that we'd better pull together for once.'

No one replied, and he started toward the door, then turned back. 'If I were you, I wouldn't spread this around for a while.'

'Why not?' asked Barksdale.

'Because we don't want any hot-headed townies organizing a posse and riding up there to chase Yaquis. We've got troubles enough without a full-scale war with the Indians. When is this crackerjack ramrod of yours coming home?' he asked.

'On tomorrow evening's train. What do you want to ask him?'

'Whether he murdered those soldiers and stole the money. It happened just about the time he took off for Bisbee.'

Barksdale grinned. 'Hope I'm around when you ask him. It ain't going to be Alden Sutton you're dealing with this time. Breen was a town marshal in Texas once.'

Logan nodded. 'So I've heard. But I thought maybe it was a town bum he used to be. Goodnight, Miss Laura. I'm serious about your moving into town. I'd do it myself, except they're holding a man and a boy I'm responsible for.'

'You're responsible for more than that, Mr. Logan,' said the girl. 'Much more. Probably for the death of those Indians, if the truth ever comes out . . .'

'If the truth ever comes out,' said Logan, 'we may, know why Barksdale left his men on guard while he was talking to you tonight.'

* * *

Barksdale and the girl heard his hoofbeats as he rode into the darkness. They sat still at the table. Laura struck her fist against the oak.

'How can he live with himself, Mr. Barksdale?' she cried. 'Such arrogance! Such accusations—!'

'He'd better go slow,' Barksdale rumbled, 'when he throws that kind of talk at Joe Breen.'

The girl angrily shook her head. 'It's perfectly obvious that he or his men killed those soldiers. I'm going to report it to the county sheriff—'

Barksdale smiled patiently and scratched his eyebrow. 'As to that, missy.' he said, 'I don't rightly believe you're in a position to back it up. You know what the sheriff would say: Logan wouldn't have come over to warn you, if he was guilty.'

'But why not? The man must have *some* feeling. He knows we'll all be slaughtered in our beds if we don't move into town.'

Barksdale reached over and patted her hand. He could feel her trembling. Her face was vivid with color; her dark hair had come unpinned here and there and its disorder was fetching.

'Tell you a secret, Miss Laura. I don't talk about this, and don't you, but I've got friends among the Yaquis. I'll be seeing them again before this so-called deadline is up. If I can't talk them into staying away from your place, I'll move you into town and push your cows up onto my range where they won't be bothered.'

Biting her lip, the girl sat back. She drew a deep sigh of anxiety, then smiled wanly. 'I wish we'd known you better when Alden was alive,' she said. 'He'd have found strength in you, I know. Instead of the humiliation he found everywhere else—'

Barksdale rose. 'Over and done with,' he sighed. 'I'll have to look for those ignorant cowhands of mine, now. They're going to find strength in me, too—right across the tops of their heads.'

CHAPTER FIVE

From the scorched hills surrounding Nogales, Tom Logan looked down on the big border town. He had passed the night at his ranch and ridden in by a trail through the foothills. Gazing at the spreading pattern of the community, he had to reach far back to remember the village his father and he used to visit when he was a boy. It was odd to be twenty-two and feeling like an old-timer.

But the old town was just a kernel now, with a husk of two-story buildings of adobe and stone around it. Out-of-plumb electric-light poles carried skinny copper vines through the town. Beyond an east-and-west-running barbed-wire barricade lay the smaller, more drab town of Mexican Nogales. But the sun fell impartially in the dusty gulches between the buildings and the miners' hovels of mud and sheet metal on the slag-like hillsides.

He rode through Nogalitos, the Mexican district, into town. These days the community closed about him with a foreign feel. It had become a merchant's and a miner's town, though a cowman could still walk tall here. It had two lawmen, a county sheriff adjusted to the way and troubles of cattlemen, and a town marshal whose specialty was saloon difficulties.

Riding in, he heard an empty wagon booming along a side street, the flat clink of a blacksmith's hammer. He left his horse at a livery stable and walked to the International Saloon, at the line, for some lunch and a beer. The cool, grotto-like saloon was thronged with businessmen having a noontime drink. A few cowboys and ranchers could be spotted among the tables—shy, taciturn, sunburned men who did not mix well and so had the reputation of being clannish.

Logan leaned against the bar and waited for service. Four bartenders in long, tube-like aprons had to move fast to keep up with the traffic. He ordered beer and a sandwich and gazed pessimistically at the new-style townsmen in the place. He had to tell Sheriff Jess Mooney what was going on, but was leery of broadcasting it among these people, many of whom had never seen an Apache, let alone a Yaqui. Town people tended to lump together mountain lions, smallpox and Indians as identical evils to be eradicated with all due speed.

An hour after he told his story, someone would be passing out tin badges and organizing a mounted posse for a punitive expedition into Mexico.

A man laid a dove-gray felt hat on the counter at Logan's elbow. 'Keep smiling, that's what I always say,' he said in a slow, melancholy voice.

Logan looked up from his sandwich. It was Sheriff Jess Mooney, calm and sad-eyed. Logan turned with relief. 'Smiling? With my troubles?' he said. 'It's a wonder I'm not in tears.'

The sheriff smoothed his sandy hair against his scalp. He was a thin, hard man who wore a gray suit and a fancy double-breasted vest with a yellow elks-tooth hanging against it. Despite his natty look, he was a cowman by birth who had ranched for years before he was elected county sheriff. The cattle country was in his tight-skinned brown face and his deliberate manner of speech.

'Troubles?' he repeated. 'Year I came here, there was smallpox, hard times, and an Indian raid every month. You wouldn't know trouble if it was wearing a baggage tag, Tom.'

Smiling, Logan cupped his hands about the sweating beer glass: 'That's just it, Jess—this trouble was wearing a tag—and the name on it was Pistola. Ever heard of him?'

Mooney, frowning, nodded slowly. 'Reckon I have.'

'Okay. Pistola's got my puncher, Julio, and his nephew. *That* kind of trouble, Jess.'

At that moment Nacho Ruiz, the proprietor, brought the sheriff's beer and set it down. Nacho was a short, burly man with a brown square face. His mustache was reddish, in contrast to his black hair. He wore a pinstriped blue suit, and a tie with a black pearl stickpin.

Laying his palms on the bar, he grinned at them.

'What's this about Pistola? Did the Dorados catch the bastard?'

Logan gave him a silent frown and turned to look out over the room. 'Let's take a table,' he muttered. He had never liked Nacho, who claimed to be related to the governor of Sonora, and made Yaqui-hating a career.

'Sorry, gentlemen, the tables are all full,' Nacho said, still smiling. 'But I'll give you the next best thing: privacy.'

He flipped the sheriff's coin, caught it, and sauntered away.

Mooney stared into Logan's eyes. 'What do you mean, he's "got" them?'

'He's holding them captive. I don't know how many men he's got with him, but it looked like a whole army.'

* * *

The sheriff pulled the bows of his reading spectacles behind his ears and examined the coin Logan showed him. In the mirror behind the bar, Logan's gaze locked momentarily with the quick, dark eyes of the saloonkeeper. Then Nacho turned away.

Damn it! Logan thought. I wish we'd gone to Mooney's office to talk . . . Mooney dealt regularly with Mexican cattlebuyers, ranchers, and cowpunchers, and his word was invariably good. But Nacho, in any language, would have rubbed him wrong. He was a climber and a hypocrite. When he laughed, only his mouth took part in the fun.

Mooney returned the coin and pulled off his spectacles. 'Were all the coins the same?'

'So the general said. Spanish—twenty *reales*.'

'Foreign gold ain't unusual, Tom. Can't jail a man for possession of it. Lots of it coming into Sonoran ports these days.'

'Not much Spanish gold, though,' Logan argued, 'and not sixty or seventy years old. If you ask me, this gold has been in the ground since Mexico split off from Spain. The padres may have buried it. Anyway, the Yaquis are using it, and it's one trail to smell along. What do you think?'

The sheriff sighed. 'I think it's damn sorry news to feed a man with his beer. How many people know about this?'

'Only Laura Sutton and Clyde Barksdale, so far. I asked them to keep it quiet, but I don't pull much weight with either of them.'

The sheriff placed his hat on his head and drew it down over his eyes; he shook his head in perplexity.

'We'd better tell this story right, Tom, or things will go sour. People in this town don't understand Indians any more. They're afraid of them. As sure as hell somebody will want to ride out there a hundred strong and hunt

Yaquis. I'll check the banks and the express office and see if they remember any big gold deposits lately. I'll talk to Breen when he gets in. That'll keep us busy for a while. Will you be in town for a day or two?'

Logan nodded. Someone moved in and swept the coin from the counter. It was Nacho again, inspecting it closely on his palm, turning it to catch the pigmented light penetrating the mock stained-glass windows in the front.

'That's a very interesting coin, gentlemen. Whose is it?'

'It's mine, and put it down,' Logan said.

Nacho laid the gold piece on the counter. He looked at Logan without expression, then at the sheriff. 'Gentlemen, what's the game?' he asked, bluntly.

'As soon as we know, Nacho, I'll tell you,' Sheriff Mooney replied.

'I didn't intend to eavesdrop, but I heard something about Pistola, Joe Breen and some captives. Check me if I'm wrong.'

Logan sighed. 'That's right, Nacho. And you keep it to hell under your hat. Leave this to the experts for a few days.'

Nacho made an angry gesture, and began talking rapidly.

'Those Goddamned Yaqui Indians! I've said it all along: let them parade up and down the Santa Cruz Valley long enough and they'll start abusing the privilege of immunity! What've they done?'

Logan winked at the sheriff. 'I've always thought you were kind of sweet on the Yaquis, Nacho,' he said.

The saloonkeeper bristled. 'What made you think that? If I've got any Indian blood, it's not Yaqui.'

'I've seen you riding into the mountains once or twice. I thought maybe you were leaving something in the mailbox for them. Once there was a note that said, "Next week would be a good time." I took it to mean the coast was clear for a crossing, because the Dorados had been in Mexican Nogales the day before, heading west.'

For an instant, Nacho's gaze faltered, then came back. 'Think what you want. All I know is that if they're raiding, the news should be passed around so that people can protect themselves.'

'In good time,' Mooney said.

'At least you're going to tell Marshal Duffy, aren't you?'

'Why should I? His jurisdiction ends at the city limits.'

Nacho eloquently raised and dropped his arms.

Outside, in the yellow blaze of midafternoon sun, the sheriff chuckled, 'You don't like that fellow much, do you?'

'No. I think he's playing both sides of the fence. If he gives the Indians a tip this month, he gives the Dorados one next.'

'Probably. But if he keeps his mouth shut for a few days, that's all we'll ask of him. I'm going to check with the banks. Why don't you look in on Bill Overton at the express office?'

* * *

Logan walked west down a rambling alley to the railroad station. The station was on the international line, which consisted of three strands of barbed wire. The tracks passed through an opening in the fence and died in the earth a few hundred yards beyond. Mexican Nogales, a low profile blurred with smoke and dust, trailed from the line a couple of miles between hillsides scarred with the cave dwellings of *descamisados*.

The Wells Fargo agency occupied one end of the railroad station. The door was locked and a cardboard clock-face on it was set at one o'clock. Logan glanced at his pocket watch and saw that it was already one-thirty. Staying in the shade under the eaves of the building, he walked to the blackboard where arrival and departures were listed. The mixed train from Bisbee and the other mining towns was due at four-thirty p.m.

He sat on a limber-legged chair, tilted it back against the wall, and relaxed. The drowsy heat collected about him. He dozed.

Suddenly, with a gasp, he flung his arms wide, fighting to recover balance. The chair legs slipped and the back of his head and shoulders scraped down the adobe wall. As his eyes snapped open, he saw two men standing near him. The chair crashed on the ground, knocking the wind out of him. He rolled aside, coming angrily awake with the clear impression of having felt a chair leg kicked an instant before the chair collapsed under him.

He came to his knees staring at the men. Bill Overton, the express agent, was sheepishly grinning as he stood swinging a key-ring. The other man, Marshal Duffy, was tall and slender in a black suit and a flat-crowned hat, a shield pinned to his vest. His shoulders filled the coat, his legs were long and straight, the heels of his boots were barbed. His jaws had a bluish shine, as though he had just shaved.

'What's the idea?' Logan said, rising slowly with his eyes on the marshal.

The marshal smiled slowly. 'Excuse me. I only meant to wake you up. Tapped your chair and over you went.'

'The next time you do that,' Logan said, 'I'm going to forget you're wearing a badge.' He picked up his hat and slapped dust from it. He watched Overton walk to the door of the express office. His mind was beginning to track now. He had little doubt that Nacho Ruiz had hustled right up to the marshal's office and told him all he knew.

'I hear you're boycotting me,' Marshal Duffy said.

'I don't know what you're talking about.'

Duffy punched his shoulder, grinning. 'Come on. You can trust me with your little secrets, cowboy.'

'More than I can say for Nacho,' Logan responded.

Overton had opened the door, and Logan followed him into a dark room with low tongue-and-groove counters and heavy wire grilles rising from counter to ceiling. The agent unlocked another door and put himself behind the counter. Against one wall, a wood stove drove a long, slanting stove-pipe into the high ceiling.

The agent glanced through a wicket as Logan approached. 'Was there something?' he asked.

Logan showed him the coin. Duffy came to stand at his elbow. 'Seen any of these lately?' Logan asked.

Overton turned the coin over, scrutinizing both sides of it. 'Real old-timer, ain't it? Maybe it's worth something.'

'It's worth a hundred to me, if I can find a man who's spending them.'

Duffy reached past the rancher. The agent put the coin in his hand. The marshal tipped his hat back and studied it. Then his glance snapped to Logan.

'And you think the man is Joe Breen. Correct?'

Logan put out his hand for the coin.

'Marshal, I've made a full report to the county sheriff. If there's anything you want to know, ask him.'

Duffy's hand dropped and he kept the gold piece. His face darkened. 'Nacho made a report to me, too. I don't care what you do out there in the woods, but what you do in town is my business, and any investigation is my business. Clear?'

'Let's have the coin,' Logan said.

Duffy surrendered the coin, but blocked his way with an outstretched hand planted against the grille. 'Some of you red-necks,' he said, 'have got the idea you own squatters' rights to this town. I'm getting sick of cowboys riding in town Saturdays to get drunk and puke on the sidewalks. You understand me?'

'Where do you want them to puke?'

'And I don't need any smart talk out of you, either,' the marshal snapped.

Now Bill Overton came into it, stabbing his finger at Logan from the security of his cage. 'If you know what's good for you, you'll leave Joe Breen alone, too! Taking the law into your own hands—Breen will make mincemeat out of you.'

'That's one worry I'll take off your mind right now,' the marshal said. 'I'll meet Breen myself and ask him any questions that are asked. The time's past when men wrote their own law in Arizona. The whole county's concerned in this, and I'll see to it they know what's going on.'

*   *   *

Logan went back to the dry heat of the platform, thinking, How stupid can you be and still pin a badge on straight? Duffy was eaten alive with jealousy. He didn't know the people, the climate, or even the insects of this borderland. A man with problems automatically found his way to Sheriff Mooney's office, had a smoke with him, and brought it out.

No wonder Duffy was jealous. All the trade he got was cowboys coming into town Saturday night to puke on the sidewalk.

CHAPTER SIX

When the train came in at four forty-five, Logan was in Sheriff Mooney's office. The only way he would get to talk to Breen, he knew, was outside of town. One of the hostlers at the stable where Breen had left his horse had promised the sheriff to bring word when Breen ordered the animal readied for the trail. Logan had brought his own horse from the stable and tied it behind the sheriff's office.

At six o'clock, the sheriff made a tour of the downtown area and returned.

'Well, he's out of sight. I checked with Marshal Duffy, and he said he wasn't on the train. But a couple of kids I talked to said he was.'

'Good. We'll track him down. I'm going down to the Pantry and get some supper. Send word if there's any news, will you?'

As he was ordering dinner, a stout man in a business suit entered and took the stool at his right. Logan recognized him as a minor official at one of the banks, a pudgy-faced man with full lips and neat gray hair. The waitress took his order and he sat back, humming to himself, one hand piano-playing on the counter as he looked the room over. His tour of inspection ended on Logan; he peered at him curiously, then smiled.

'Say, you're—' He snapped his fingers as he searched for the name.

'Tom Logan.'

'Sure, sure. How're you, Logan? I'm King, from the Stockmen's Bank. How's the cattle business?'

'*Poco, poco,*' Logan said. 'How's banking?'

'The same.'

Their food came. Logan had the strong feeling that King had sought him out, that he had something to say but was not ready to say it.

'Aren't you married?' Logan asked.

King glanced up. 'Married? My God, yes. That hole in my nose is where the ring goes through. Why?'

'If I were married, I'd eat at home,' Logan smiled.

'Wife's away.'

King ate greedily as they talked, stuffing quantities of fried potatoes in his mouth and getting grease on his chin. When he had finished, he wiped his mouth and chin on the big linen napkin, signaled the waitress and tapped his coffee cup, then leaned back.

'You collect coins?' he asked.

Logan felt a bristling of excitement. But looking at King, he shook his head. 'Just money in general. Why?'

'Sheriff Mooney was in this afternoon trying to find examples of a certain type of Spanish coin. Said if we turned up any, to tell him or you.'

Logan asked quickly: 'Have you found some?'

Taking a fork from the counter, King commenced scraping under his nails. 'I've collected oddities for years, ever since I was a kid. Gold's my specialty—gold dollars, quarter-eagles—'

'How about foreign gold? Say, twenty *reales*. Spanish?'

A smile touched King's full lips. 'Any special year?'

'Oh—1810,1820.'

King dug into a vest pocket, worked out a large golden coin, and laid it on the counter.

'Like this, maybe?'

Logan picked it up, his mouth going dry and his pulse thudding. 'Like that. Yes, sir. That's the kind I collect. Where'd you find it?'

'In my safety deposit box, where I put it a couple of weeks ago. Remembered it had come in with a deposit from some merchant or other, so I looked back through the slips. It was from the railroad ticket office, deposited by Harry Drew. Harry was in just before quitting time today with the receipts, and I asked him if he remembered where he got it.'

Logan gripped his arm. 'Good! What'd he say?'

King sipped his coffee, milking the moment of all the drama it contained.

'To be truthful, Logan, Marshal Duffy was in today, too. I got more of the story from him than I did from Sheriff Mooney. Otherwise I wouldn't have gone to all this trouble. Both of them wanted to be told about anything we found. But we aren't called the Stockmen's Bank for nothing—our business was founded on cattle. Besides, Duffy moved his account to the Miner's Bank because we wouldn't let him use his savings accounts as a checking account without charge.'

'Okay. What'd Drew say?' Logan pleaded.

Patting his lips with the soiled napkin, King leaned closer. 'Harry said Joe Breen used it to buy a ticket to Bisbee two weeks ago.'

Logan laid down fifty cents for his meal and

stood up. 'Will you sell me that coin, King? Twenty dollars for twenty *reales*?'

'Sure. But you're losing money. It's only worth ten, at the current exchange rate.'

'To me,' Logan said, 'it may be worth ten thousand. Here—scratch your initials on it, will you? I'll turn it over to the sheriff later.'

He counted out twenty dollars, while the banker used the tip of a penknife blade to etch his initials into the coin. Logan then put the coin in a sack of Bull Durham for safe keeping.

'By the way,' King said, 'I just saw Breen's horse in front of the International Saloon. Stopped in to tell the sheriff, but he was out somewhere . . .'

* * *

It occurred to Logan that there might be an advantage in entering the saloon unexpectedly. He walked out the back to the alley, then turned south toward the rear of the saloon. In the alley, a buzzard was feasting on the carcass of a dead dog. It flapped up to a parapet roof as he passed.

In a vacant lot behind the saloon were a four-place backhouse, pyramids of empty whiskey and beer casks, and a midden of trash. He opened a door frame screened with mosquito bar and looked down a short hall ending in a curtain. On either side was a door. He walked down the hall and pushed the curtain aside sufficiently to survey the room.

The big room was crowded with men having an afterwork drink. These days he scarcely recognized anyone in the International. On a good evening its patrons might include a couple of mining promoters, a few Army officers, and some commercial travelers, in addition to the local merchants and ranchers. A mechanical monstrosity in a far corner, a great box of walnut and glass, was giving out a horrendous wheezing, pumping, and crashing of musical instruments hitched to pipes and tubes. Voices pierced it confusedly; a businesslike murmur from a table of merchants near the back, drunken laughter from the bar. His gaze searched through the room. He saw Judge Fowley, the corpulent, red-faced customshouse broker, seated with a couple of Mexican businessmen and another American.

Then his traveling gaze halted at the next table. Joe Breen was sitting there drinking beer with Nacho Ruiz. Logan parted the curtain and went into the bar.

Moving through the tables, he thought of the Yaqui funeral party bearing the two dead soldiers. By now they would have reached a village where there was holy ground in which to lay them. A religious and proud people—a race beyond the comprehension of men like Joe Breen. The foreman was tipped back in his chair. He wore tight black pants and a yellow vest; his tumbs were hooked in his vest pockets. He had long horse-like features, and now the lidded eyes arrogantly surveyed the room. Logan catalogued the things wrong with the man: the heavy yellow hair was mane-like, his sideburns were too long, and he wore two pearl-handled Colts. What ramrod needed two guns? They were merely showpieces to impress the kind of girl he could have bought for a dollar anyway. At the same time, he could probably use them effectively, and it was Logan's cue to see that he had no opportunity to draw them.

Reaching, the table, Logan saw to his satisfaction that Breen was sitting too close to it to draw the guns easily. The long, yellow-haired ramrod was watching a girl straighten the seam of her stocking a few tables away. He started, as a coin chimed on the table before him and danced a golden tune before ringing down. He looked up at Logan, questioningly.

Nacho Ruiz put his hand over the coin, his broad face darkening. 'My God, are you still running around showing that damned coin?'

Logan moved around to Breen's right. When the foreman tried to push his chair back, Logan placed his boot on a rung and blocked it.

'How was the trip?' he asked.

'Great,' Breen said. 'Let's see the coin,' he said to the saloonkeeper.

While Breen looked at the gold piece,

Logan said: 'Spring's a hell of a time to take a pleasure trip, isn't it?'

Breen did not look up. Despite his calmness, Logan knew he was gathering himself mentally and physically.

'Who said it was pleasure?' Breen shrugged.

'What kind of business has a cowman got in a mining town?'

'None of yours, that's for damned sure,' Breen retorted.

'Where'd you get the coin?'

'Never saw it before. What's the matter, your brains getting baked out there in the mesquite?'

'Harry Drew says you bought your train ticket with that coin. How many more have you got?'

Nacho slapped the coin on the table with a sudden gesture and stood up.

'Get out of here!' he shouted at Logan. 'I won't tolerate people provoking fights in my place. He's been talking it all over town that you killed and robbed a couple of Yaqui Indians, Joey!' he told Breen. 'I said, "Why not wait till Joe's here to defend himself?" '

Logan smiled, keeping his eyes on Breen. 'That's what I'm doing, Nacho. Waiting for Joey to defend himself . . .'

Suddenly the saloonkeeper reached down and seized a short length of pool cue which had been propped against his chair, out of view. Logan swung a swift backhand blow to

Ruiz's face that drove him back. He saw a flash of movement from Breen and turned hastily.

A heavy beer glass struck him on the forehead, stunning him. His knees buckled; he slipped to the floor. Blood flowed over one eye and down his cheek.

Above him, Breen was kicking the chair back and rising. Logan reached out and seized a spurred boot and twisted it savagely with both hands. Breen yelled and threw himself to the floor to stop the twisting pressure on his ankle. Immediately he came to his knees. Logan picked up the beer schooner, while blood ran over his shirtfront and dripped from his chin. His arm cocked as Breen started to rise; he threw it with full strength. With a loud thump, the glass struck Breen in the chest. He sat down with a gasp.

Logan looked up. Nacho had vanished; men were sinking beneath the tables, and a bartender was yelling.

'Now, boys! Now, boys!'

Breen stumbled to his feet, dazed. Logan scrambled up. His eyes still clouded, the foreman dropped his right hand over his gun, more in a gesture of defense than of threatening. Logan quickly took hold of a chair.

You botched it up good! he thought, startled, watching Breen's face to try to anticipate what he was going to do.

Without warning, Breen pulled the gun.

Logan hurled the chair at his head. Breen raised his gun arm to ward off the chair and took the weight of it against his forearm. He swore and fell back. The gun pinwheeled brightly and landed butt-first on the floor.

There was a flash and a roar, as the Colt fired and skidded away under the tables. A cloud of bitter gray powder smoke rolled over Logan. He was so stunned by the concussion and the flash that for an instant he thought he had been hit.

Then he heard a man moaning.

'Boys, I think—I think I've been—'

The voice came from Judge Fowley's table; it sounded like the judge's voice. Logan moved cautiously toward the foreman, not daring to take his gaze from him. Breen's face reflected shock at the sight of the rancher's cut face and blood-soaked shirt. He took a step backward, and his left hand began to stray toward his gun.

Logan lunged into him.

Breen failed to draw the gun before Logan collided with him. He took a solid punch high on the forehead which knocked him back into a table. A second blow crushed his lower lip against his teeth. Hurt and bleeding, he fell aside. Logan caught him with a short, driving punch to the heart which brought a pained gasp from Breen's lips and sent him staggering into another table. As the man started to fall, Logan caught him and held him up. He swung a roundhouse right to snap the yellow-haired ramrod's head back and drop him. Breen rolled over on his face, came into a crawling posture, and collapsed.

A quiet spread through the barroom. Panting, Logan heard spurs chiming. A hand fell on his shoulder and wrenched him around. Marshal Duffy stood there, a Colt in his hand. His face was an angry red.

'What did I tell you, Goddamn it?' he raged. 'Didn't I tell you to let me handle things?' He shoved Logan away and turned to Judge Fowley's table. 'Who's hurt?' he asked quickly.

A man said: 'It's Judge Fowley, Marshal. Reckon he's quit.'

Duffy groaned. He bent over the old man lying half under the table, then straightened quickly and gazed down at Joe Breen. Then he turned and in sudden rage shoved the barrel of the Colt in Logan's face.

'If I don't make an example of you—so help me God! If I don't throw the Goddamn book at you!'

CHAPTER SEVEN

The room of Nacho Ruiz, upstairs above the International Saloon, was on the east side of the building. Mornings, the desert sun glared fiercely against the windows, so Nacho kept the faded heavy purple drapes drawn and the windows closed. Very little heat penetrated the thick adobe walls, and if the night were cool the room remained comfortable all the next day. By midafternoon, the sun blazed against the west side of the building like a torch. But those were the girls' rooms.

At eleven a.m., Joe Breen heard Nacho climbing the narrow flight of stairs to the room. The foreman lay on Nacho's bed with two pillows propping him up, a cigarette held lazily in his lips. He twirled his Colt by the trigger guard. He had taken the liberty of opening the curtains and gazed sleepily at the window. Through the wavy glass he could see the potato-shaped green hills behind Mexican Nogales. Breen's left eye was completely closed; a barber's leech clung to the pendulous upper lid. His lower lip was fantastically swollen and there was a gap where he had lost a lower front tooth. Minor cuts and bruises marred the rest of his face. He wore his tight black pants, but no shirt. He had a white pigeon-like chest with no noticeable hair.

Nacho opened the door and came in. The short barrel-chested Mexican in his natty striped suit shook his head.

'Jesus, did you have to open the curtains?' he muttered. 'The room's like a furnace.'

'I hate curtains. They make me think of a funeral parlor. What's the word?'

Nacho dropped into a deep leather chair

and took a black Spanish cigar from a humidor that smelled like rum. 'The coroner's jury will sit at two o'clock. Logan's out on bail. Clyde Barksdale's roaming around looking for you,' he added.

'Did he ask where I was?'

'No—I ducked when I saw him coming, and the bartenders don't know where you are. How you feeling?'

'Mean,' said the foreman. 'Mean.' He gave the cylinder of his Colt a clicking spin with the palm of his free hand.

Nacho dropped the match in a coffee cup and walked to the bed. 'How's that leech doin'? Swelling coming down any?'

'Not much.'

Nacho touched the slimy flat worm, whose body was like soft black rubber. 'He ain't started to work yet. Maybe he don't like whiskey in his food,' he grinned.

Breen tossed the cigarette out the window. 'Seen Logan around?'

Nacho, sitting down again, said: 'No. Take my advice and forget about him. Win one, lose one. They'll hold a hearing, decide it was accidental death, and wipe it out. But if you kill Logan now, you'll probably be hung.'

Breen touched a cut on his cheekbone and winced. 'You've got it backwards: lose one, win one, and I've got a win coming up. Logan won't have me jammed under the table next time.'

'What are you going to tell Sheriff Mooney about that coin?' Nacho asked.

The gun cylinder rasped as Breen spun it again. 'That I got it in some change.'

'You know,' Nacho said mildly, 'that was a stupid thing to do—use one of the coins that way. You were taking a big risk to hold out any of them when you cached them—let alone spend one.'

Breen shrugged. 'What can they prove?'

'Let's not fool ourselves, Joselito. This barrel of snakes you're wading around in could begin to strike, *prontito.* Tom Logan poking in it the way he is—that ain't going to help.'

'That's one reason I'm going to close the books on him,' Breen said.

'It's the reason you're *not*,' Nacho said forcefully. 'It would be too Goddamn obvious. Leave him alone. They'll make an investigation into the judge's death and you're bound to be cleared. Then, before Mooney can start asking questions about them Yaquis, you'd better tell people you're sick of this town, and grab a train. *After* we make our split . . .'

'Don't get in a rush,' Breen drawled. 'First I deal with Logan. Then I deal with you.'

The saloonkeeper puffed quietly on the cigar, drew it from his lips and picked a scrap of tobacco from his tongue. He smiled at Breen.

'You *did* kill them Yaquis, though,

Joselito—you and Clyde Barksdale. And if I was you, I'd be hightailing it before my luck ran out.'

Breen, spinning the gun cylinder again, turned the weapon so that it pointed at Nacho. Nacho half closed his eyes, his mouth tightening.

'Can you *prove* we killed them?' Breen asked.

'Move that gun off me,' Nacho said sharply. Breen rocked the hammer twice, but, with a little sigh, turned the barrel aside.

'You seemed to think I could prove it,' Nacho added, 'when you offered to cut me in. It's all wrote down, too. I told you that. So don't get loose with your guns, *compadre*.'

Breen was a stranger to frustration. Direct action had been his lifelong code. To be thwarted in anything caused a souring of his whole being, roused a crazy urge to strike in all directions until he was out of the corner. Nacho was one of the first long-term frustrations he had had to deal with, but the Mex had him laced up like a calf for branding. The funny thing was—and Breen obscurely resented it—Clyde Barksdale didn't even know they were under the thumb of the Mexican saloonkeeper!

It showed how foolish it was to try to plan anything. If you were going to do it, do it. Barksdale had probably been scheming this for years. Breen was dealing poker in El Paso when Barksdale told him he could put him in a job as foreman of an Arizona ranch, with a big chance of making a killing. Experience no object.

Six months after he took the job, the chance to make a killing suddenly broke.

Barksdale explained about these Yaqui soldiers and the money they occasionally lugged up to Tucson. It was easy to spot a treasure train, because otherwise the Indians traveled afoot and without pack animals. Barksdale would watch for them, and the two of them would knock over the Indians and bury the money. After a few weeks they would quietly split it. It would be too heavy to divide up like a cake and everybody eat his share. Would have to be packed out or removed a bit at a time.

Everything went fine. They killed the Indians just at dusk and buried the gold in an old mine on Mrs. Sutton's land. Barksdale didn't want it on his, because if the Yaquis *should* smell it out—well, everybody knew they were meaner than a bucket of red ants.

Then, as Breen was riding home in the dark, Nacho popped up.

He'd seen it all. Nacho, now and then, left messages and supplies for the Yaquis in a cave on Tom Logan's land—keeping his fences mended. He'd been in the brush that day and had seen the murder . . . So Nacho suggested they move the gold to a new hiding place. At the proper time, they would split it. Breen agreed.

What else could he do, while Nacho's rifle was pointed at him?

The next day he was supposed to take the train to Bisbee to be out of the area while the bodies were found and things began to pop. Barksdale knew Yaquis, could handle himself when they called on him, but it would be safer for Breen to be away.

That day, as he got on the train, Nacho handed him a letter.

Reading it later, the foreman learned that Nacho's death would automatically cause a certain document to be opened among his effects . . .

It mattered little to Breen whom he split with, actually. Barksdale was giving him only a third of the take. With Ruiz, the cut was down the middle. Nevertheless, he didn't want to cut and run, now, the way Nacho was talking about.

'Gimme a few days,' Breen said. 'Maybe I'll think of something.'

'Okay,' Nacho said. 'We don't have to decide now. The inquest's going to be in an hour. Better clean up. Don't wear a gun, and don't go there dressed like a pimp. Hey?' He winked and stood up.

'Hey,' Breen muttered, thinking: Maybe I'll have to do something about you too, you greasy little . . .

CHAPTER EIGHT

The coroner's inquest was held in the basement of the courthouse, a steep and narrow stone building with high, arched windows and doors. The jury sat in a damp, low-ceilinged room with rough cement floors and walls frosty with lime. Tom Logan sat with Sheriff Mooney among the witnesses. Among the spectators were Laura Sutton and Clyde Barksdale. Logan was conscious of hard looks directed his way from townspeople.

For an hour the jury listened to testimony, filing into another room, once, to view the corpse, then adjourning to confer. While they awaited the verdict, the spectators talked in low voices, fanned themselves, and ate sandwiches they had brought. Laura Sutton sat primly, expressing no emotion and never once looking at Logan. For her, this was her second inquest in less than a year.

She must think it's a wild country, thought Logan, *and me the wildest animal in it.* Gazing at her, he felt sorry for the girl—sorry for what had happened between him and her brother. He knew she was scared and had been badly hurt by all that had taken place. Most of all, perhaps, by her conviction that people regarded her, and had regarded her brother, as a weaker breed of human being.

For her own good, she should sell out and go home. The fact that she did not showed that she was less different from this rough-haired Western breed than she thought.

As he was studying her, her eyes moved slightly and they were gazing at each other. Logan felt his skin become goose-flesh as her gaze was turned upon him. For some reason that he did not understand, he smiled faintly. He was trying to say, I'm not so bad as it looks, Laura—you're in this as much as I am, if you only knew it.

Instantly, she looked away. Color tinged her cheeks. And now it was Barksdale who, sensing the encounter, turned his black, cinder-hard stare on the rancher. Their eyes locked, and Logan put all his dislike and suspicion into his face. How much do you know about those Yaquis?—he wondered. You hired Breen for her. What's your part in this?

The jury returned.

'We find the death of Judge Fowley to have been accidental, caused by—'

There was a low, indignant muttering from the spectators. The judge thumped his desk with the blunt end of a pencil. 'Let's have it quiet in here. Continue, Mr. Foreman.'

The foreman concluded the findings and sat down. Joe Breen flicked a cigarette at a cuspidor, missed it, and stood up with a wink at Nacho Ruiz, among the witnesses.

'Just a minute,' a man said. It was Marshal

Duffy, rising broad-shouldered and somber from his seat and walking forward to scowl at Breen and Logan and then face the jury.

'What is it, Marshal?' asked the judge.

Duffy cleared his throat, a little habit he had when he was irritated. 'I'm not trying to tell the jury how to run its business,' he said, 'but I want to put something in the record. I warned Tom Logan to leave the questioning of Joe Breen to me. If he'd followed orders, Judge Fowley would still be alive. So if he isn't criminally responsible for his death, he sure as the devil didn't help much to keep him alive!'

Suddenly people were clapping. Angry affirmations were called from the benches, and the judge banged on the desk with his palm. 'That's enough of that!' When it was quiet, he said, 'Marshal, that may be true, but it don't have any bearing on the manner of Judge Fowley's death, so we can't put it in the record.'

'*But*,' he said, turning his eyes to Logan, 'I'm going to tell this young man something, and I want him to remember it. This is not the half-broke town it was ten years ago, when he was growing up. We've got a municipal water system, we've got doctors, we've got a fire department *and* we've got two full-time lawmen. Either one of those officers can issue an order which he must obey, or take the consequences. Now, it may very well be that in disobeying Marshal Duffy's instructions, he committed a misdemeanor. I'll ask the city attorney to look into that.'

Marshal Duffy put his hand in his pocket, stared briefly at Logan, and started down the aisle between the benches. But now Sheriff Mooney was rising from Logan's side.

'Just a minute, Marshal,' he said.

There was a tightening of the air in the chamber. The town knew of the rivalry between the officers and they leaned forward expectantly to hear what Sheriff Mooney's rebuttal would be.

'May I speak, Your Honor?' Mooney asked. His voice was quiet and slow.

'Go ahead, Sheriff.'

'I wanted to keep this news quiet for a while; but it seems to be already out. A man was in my office this morning wanting me to deputize a body of men to hunt Yaquis. All of you know what I'm talking about. I just want to remind folks that, so far, all the murdering's been on our side. We don't know who did the killing, but it's my job to try to find out. It's Tom Logan's too, since he and a number of other ranchers are going to have to quit ranching if we don't make time on this. Otherwise they'll be massacred.'

Logan saw that the girl was gazing intently at Mooney. She appeared to be taking his warning more seriously than she had his own.

'Tom Logan was trying to ask Joe Breen the same question I plan to ask him,' the sheriff concluded. 'Namely, where did he get that coin? There was no reason for Breen to draw his gun.'

'All right,' the judge said. 'You're at liberty to arrest Mr. Breen if you want to run the risk of false arrest. However—speaking of coins—' He turned on the chair, reached into his pocket and spilled a jingling handful of change onto his desk.

'I seem to have some foreign gold right here,' he said, smiling. Adjusting his spectacles, he went through the coins. 'As long as our own Treasury Department doesn't see fit to provide us with currency, we'll just have to make do with foreign money. Let me see—here's an English half crown—a couple of French coins—and by George, here's a Spanish coin! Four *reales*.'

'What year, Your Honor?' Tom Logan called.

The judge scrutinized the coin. 'Looks like, uh—1877.'

'Coins like that are common,' said Logan. 'But there hasn't been any old Spanish gold floating around for as long as I can remember. Mexico split off seventy years ago, and she's had her own currency ever since.'

The judge stood up, shaking his head. 'This is not what the jury was convened to decide. It's an entirely different matter, and perhaps it's one that should be explored thoroughly. Personally, I tend to discount this Yaqui threat as a bugaboo. The Indians can't *afford* to get out of line in this country.'

'They can't afford to lose ten thousand dollars, either,' Logan replied.

The judge looked out over the room. 'Adjourned,' he said.

Joe Breen sauntered to the court reporter's table, where his revolver—the one which had killed Judge Fowley—lay with a tag on the trigger guard. Breen tore off the tag and flipped out the loading gate. Then he loaded the Colt and dropped it into his holster. With his hands on the butts of his guns, he gazed for a moment with his single good eye at Logan; then he started up the aisle.

Barksdale and Laura Sutton were waiting for him. Logan heard her saying something about his injuries; then the shuffling of the spectators filing out muffled their voices. He waited with the sheriff until the room had almost cleared. Mooney got up, his brown, ropy features stern. They started out.

'Tom, I think you'd be safer at the ranch than you'll be around here for a couple of days,' the sheriff said.

'You're talking about Breen?' Logan muttered.

'I'm talking about two or three dozen men. The way it looks to me, people are inclined to lump you with the Yaquis right now. The old judge was well-liked. And Duffy was right: you should have left it to him.'

Logan frowned. Maybe it was one of those remarks a man in public office had to make. But he had gotten in a few licks at Breen, and the gunman had some more coming—until he explained the coincidences of his trip, that coin, and the Yaqui killings.

Mooney was muttering, 'I'll do what I can to clear things up. I'll get the paper to run a story on the murder. And I'll talk it up so that every man in town will be looking at the gold in his pocket and finding out that it was more than coincidence that Breen had that gold piece.'

'Are you going to question him?'

Mooney nodded. 'I told the stableman to hold his horse so he couldn't take off. If I learn anything, I'll let you know.'

Logan walked back to the sheriff's office to get his horse. He waited a few minutes, but the sheriff and Breen did not appear. He knew the lawman was right about the possibility of trouble. Pour a few drinks into some of the men who had been at the hearing, and they'd change personality, finding courage and anger to make a move they would never have made, sober.

He stopped at a Mexican store in Nogalitos, the Mexican shack town on the road out of town, and made a few purchases. As he was tucking them into his saddlebags, he heard a horse clopping up the road and a grinding of buggy tires in the earth; looking up, he saw a light, umbrella-topped buggy approaching.

The horse's legs threw long, crisscrossing shadows on the road. It was Laura Sutton's yellow-wheeled town buggy, and the girl sat alone under the umbrella.

He saw her pull the horse in as she recognized him. Then, realizing it was too late to turn aside, she shook the lines and sent the horse on faster. Turning his stirrup to mount, Logan felt a tingling. One part of his mind dictated, sternly, *Pay no attention to her.* That would bother her worse than anything. Another part said, more forcefully: *Ride with her. She can't be that pretty and be completely foolish. Maybe you can talk some sense to her.*

He swung up, but delayed moving out, as he pretended to adjust a rein which had become twisted. From the shadow of his hat brim he studied the slender figure in the small, impractical buggy. He felt sorry for her—sorry he could not have been a friend instead of a nuisance at the start, and finally, an enemy. And, somehow, sorry that despite everything the prospect of being with her could make him tingle and feel as awkward as a colt.

He squeezed the horse with his knees as the buggy passed, moving in beside her.

She continued gazing straight ahead. 'It's going to be dark before you reach home, Miss Laura,' he said. 'Shouldn't be out alone in this kind of weather.'

She glanced at the ragged skyline. 'It doesn't look particularly threatening, Mr.

Logan.'

'That's where our weather's deceptive—I mean Indian weather. It's always threatening.'

'Oh—'

'If you don't mind, I'll ride along to my turnoff,' he suggested, and listened for her refusal.

She glanced down, then up at the road again. 'All right,' she murmured.

He was surprised at the quick, warm pleasure he felt. For a time the *chunk, chunk, chunk* of their horses' hoofs was the only sound. 'I reckon animals like me ought to stay out of town,' he said. 'We always get excited by the traffic and get in a mess.'

'Perhaps you should.'

The thin curtain hanging between them, which had kept them from seeing one another clearly for two years, was still in place somehow. He wanted to say something conciliatory—to reach her.

'You look—very nice,' he said. 'Nice and cool,' he added, clumsily.

She faced him quickly. Her brows drew in; she started to make some impatient reply, then looked away.

His ear itched and he dug at it. 'I wish I'd have gotten off to a better start with your brother,' he said. 'At first, I thought we were going to hit it off fine. He had a—a real nice way, knew the right thing to say. At least when he was—'

He bit his tongue. The unspoken word, *sober*, clanged in the air between them. Laura drew a breath and looked at him. 'Please—!' she said.

Touched with irritation, he replied: 'All right. Let's bring it up to date. Are you really sold on that ramrod of yours?'

'I think he's fine.'

'Let me tell you a couple of things about him. In the first place, he doesn't know one blamed thing about range management. There's patches of your best pasture he's let the cows graze down to bedrock, and now rattleweed's taking it over. Rattleweed will kill cattle, you know. Or maybe you didn't know. Maybe you'd like rattleweed—it has a pretty blue flower, like lupine. Once it gets established, nothing but burning will clear it, and then you've got to buy and scatter seed—and hope.'

She hesitated, and he knew she had wondered about those pretty blue patches the cattle liked to browse in, staying there even after there was no graze left, so that they lost flesh and acted strangely dazed.

'What should I do about it?' she said.

'Have some of those shiftless cowhands Breen's hired make trusses of good range hay and drag them around on the bare spots and where the rattleweed's growing. Wait 'til the seed's ripe, though. It'll come back.'

'Very interesting. What else is he doing?'

'Well, he can't judge calves, of course. He makes beef calves out of the ones you ought to keep for breeding. In two years, a foreman like that can break a ranch.'

She shrugged. 'I don't pretend to know these things. That's why I'm in the position I am. But how can I trust anyone. Mr. Barksdale had been very helpful, and I have no reason not to trust him—'

'None, except that he's a freighter instead of a rancher. And he's going broke, too. He's overgrazing, and unless he sells off some of his herd or buys more land, he's going to have to feed those cows of his or he won't have any beef to sell next fall. Figure it out: so many cows to the section. Ask your banker and cattle-buyer—ask anybody. They may not agree on anything else, but they'll agree on that. Ask right away—you're doing the same thing.'

On a hillside from which they could gaze out to the eastern horizon, they stopped to rest the horses. Against a clear, pale evening sky, the ranks of grayish-pink hills were bare and ribbed with shadow; a breeze blew from the river and the air was quiet, cool, and serene. For a while they were silent. He knew she was appreciating the beauty of it, and he was glad; many easterners never did learn to see the beauty of a border landscape.

The girl smiled. 'Now let's talk about you,' she said.

'Fine.'

'Doesn't it even seem significant that you get involved in so much trouble? Isn't it possible you're looking for it, without meaning to?'

Logan sighed. 'Laura, I've given that a lot of thought. I think maybe I've caught trouble, like you'd catch the measles. Take your brother: I always tried to give him room—stay out of his way. But he always manged to rub me where the skin's thin. The first time I met him, he called me "young man," and told me to hold his horse while he went into a store—the horse wasn't fully broke, he said. Shoot, it was plumb wore out. But you see, he *told* me, he didn't ask me. Now, that doesn't go down with a loner like me. So I walked off and left him.'

Laura smiled, looking genuinely pleased. 'He had a bad habit of doing that. I'm happy that you have more sensitivity than I gave you credit for.'

'I've got plenty of that,' Logan grinned. 'I'm as sensitive as a sandpapered snake.'

She laughed softly, and drove on.

It was dark when they came to the place where Logan turned northeast toward his headquarters. His horse tried to head for the barn and he held it.

'I think I'd better ride the rest of the way with you,' he said.

'Do you really think the country's suddenly

become so dangerous?'

'In a way,' Logan said, 'I wish I were in your position instead of mine. As soon as you're convinced of what I'm trying to tell you, you can go into town and stay there 'til it's safe. But I've got to ride back to the Yaquis. If I've got the money they lost, fine. If I haven't, I'll die along with Julio and his nephew.'

Laura's face, shadowed but softly lit by a frosting of moon, was sober. 'I've been told by enough people who should know that I believe it now. What I don't believe is that my foreman had anything to do with it.'

Logan's horse pricked up its ears. Faintly, a moment later, he heard horses. 'If he didn't,' he returned, 'he was standing mighty close to somebody who did. I don't believe that Spanish coin was an accident. And I might as well tell you. I intend to talk to him.'

The girl shook the lines and nodded impersonally. 'Goodnight. Thank you for seeing me home.'

'Goodnight.'

He knew it was Barksdale and Breen behind them. As soon as possible, he dropped into a sandy wash and walked his horse up it in the moonlight. He carried his rifle in his free hand. He stopped finally and listened. The hoof-beats had faded. But he continued to carry the rifle, cocked and off safety. This country was becoming as elemental as it had been during the Apache times a few years ago.

CHAPTER NINE

Barksdale had hoped, but not really expected, to overtake Tom Logan. This was Logan's country, and he was part of it; touch the animal at one end, and the other end knew about it. The big freighter was somber with dissatisfaction. Too many things had happened which need not have happened.

After they passed Logan's cutoff, he told Joe Breen: 'Where were you before the hearing? I looked all over hell.'

'I used a room at the saloon,' Breen said.

'Nacho's?'

'Yep.'

'Stay away from that little chili-picker,' said Barksdale. 'I don't trust him. Not a nickel's worth.'

'Nacho didn't know I was there, even. The bartender said there was this room under the stairs I could stay in till I felt better.'

Barksdale peered at him, then seemed to accept the explanation. 'How you feeling?' he asked.

Breen snapped his fingers. His long face, bruised and swollen, smoldered with inner heat. 'Good. Like action.'

'Little more action and you'll be dead. You didn't tell me you held out some of them Spanish coins when we buried them.'

Breen shrugged. 'Only that one.'

'How'd you get hold of it?' When we buried the coins in that mine, we didn't open the packs.'

Breen turned his head sharply. 'Maybe you better put a Pinkerton detective on me, Clyde. We opened the packs at Logan's line-camp, after we killed the Indians—remember? And scattered a few in the brush for Pistola to find after he'd dug up the bodies. Well, I held one out as a keepsake, and I used it to buy the ticket because we were splitting the cost of it. I didn't know it was a freak. So quit it. I'm trying to think.'

Barksdale relaxed with a chuckle. 'You Fancy Dan gunmen,' he said. 'You're all twittery and nerved up, like sparrows.' But he felt better. He had feared, hearing about the coin, that Breen might have been dipping into the money—riding out there and moving part of it, even. But Breen's explanation was convincing.

They reached Logan's turnoff. Sitting on their horses, they listened to the night sounds: the whisper of wind through some frayed sotol spears, the cry of a night hawk. Barksdale dismounted, struck a match, and inspected the ground.

He dropped the match and straightened. 'Good. He rode off to his own place. Wonder if they were together?'

'What's the difference?'

'He might sweet-talk her. If she stops walking the line I set her, there might be a little trouble.'

Remounting, Barksdale headed on down the county road toward the ranch. 'You coming with me?' Breen asked, surprised.

'Got to talk to Miss Laura. She's going to help us square up with Logan.'

'*Help* us?' Breen snorted: 'I don't need no help.'

'Hell you don't. You can ride out and kill him, and I'll see you hung a month from now. Or you can do it my way—have some fun and see him crawl. And I promise you, Joey-boy, he won't be bothering us any more! I didn't study under the Yaquis for nothing!'

* * *

When they reached the Sutton ranch, Laura was in the kitchen with two of the servants. Barksdale tapped on the screen door and the girl glanced out through the screen.

'Oh—Mr. Barksdale,' she said. 'Is everything all right?'

'Fine, fine. That's what *I* came to ask *you*.'

She opened the screen door and smiled at him. 'I'm all right, thank you. Is Joe with you?'

Hat in hand, Barksdale nodded. 'He's gone to the bunkhouse to lay down. Thought it might be best to ride out with him to make sure he got here all right. Logan gave him a real drubbin'.'

Laura bit her lip, glancing down. 'Mr. Barksdale, I have to tell you something. Mr. Logan rode with me part way tonight.'

Barksdale nodded. 'I know. Saw your tracks.'

'We had a very good talk. I was quite encouraged—'

'In what way?' asked the freighter, politely.

'Encouraged to think there might be a way out of our difficulties.'

Barksdale's large, rough head nodded. 'Been thinking the same thing. Stuff goes from bad to worse, don't it? Well what I was thinking—' He broke off, chewing the corner of his mustache.

'Yes?'

'That we might have a three-way talk, you and me and Logan. Get together someplace halfway between all our ranches—say the old Monk place—and talk everything over.'

'I'd like it very much,' Laura said enthusiastically.

'Good. Do you want to write a little note? You can sign it, I'll sign underneath, and we'll send it over by my Mexican. What about one o'clock tomorrow afternoon?'

Laura extended her hand, smiling. 'Splendid! Come inside while I write the note.'

After she had written the letter, she signed it. Barksdale seated himself and laid his left forearm across the page as though it might escape. Then, using great muscular effort, he drove the unfamiliar writing instrument to its work of fashioning his name. He hesitated, glanced at the letter, and made a small stroke in the body of the writing.

'Missed a comma,' he said, and chuckled at his joke.

With a curlicue, he had changed Laura's *one o'clock* to *six o'clock*.

He folded the letter and crammed it into the envelope. When he licked the flap, she glanced away with a slight frown of distaste.

'There,' he said, rising and tucking the envelope into his shirt pocket. 'I'll be at the Monk place a little before one. You might as well come alone and not take Joe from his work. You'll be back before dark, I expect. I'll send Chaparro over with the letter tonight.'

* * *

Although they waited until nearly three o'clock the following afternoon, Tom Logan did not appear.

For an hour Laura passed the time in an activity which both amused Barksdale and appalled him with its utter nonsensicality. She painted watercolors of wild flowers.

She had brought along a paint box and drawing tablet in a big tapestry bag, and settled herself on one of the ruined walls of the old Monk ranch house to paint. Chaparro, whom Barksdale had brought with him, filled a rusty tin can with water at her direction, and she arranged the tiny pastel-tinted flowers in it.

'They wither in minutes without water,' Laura explained to the freighter. 'They're so delicate. But I love them.'

'You ain't fooling me, Missy,' Barksdale said. 'You want to look fashionable for young Logan when he shows up—ain't that so?'

Her cheeks grew pink while she denied it. 'It's of no interest to me whether Mr. Logan thinks I look "fashionable." Don't be silly, Clyde. It is getting late though, isn't it?'

He said it was nearly two, and studied the long sweep of stone and grass running down to the foothills where Logan had his home place. 'He'll be along. We wind our clocks different in this country than you did in the East.'

'Ask Chaparro if he *definitely* delivered my letter,' Laura suggested.

Barksdale spoke to the little Mexican, and Chaparro spoke earnestly to the girl in reply.

'Si! Si, señorita. Lo hizo, de vera.'

'Says he done it for sure,' Barksdale interpreted.

But at three o'clock, when Laura had painted every scrap of weed in sight, she rinsed her brushes, closed the box, and announced quietly:

'He's not coming, Clyde.'

'I reckon not. I'll see you home.'

'It's not necessary.'

Frowning, he insisted. 'No time for young females to be running around alone. Chaparro, head for home,' he said.

As he placed himself by her horse so that she could use his knee as a mounting block, she said wistfully, 'I really believed what he said about wanting no trouble. He could at least have done us the courtesy of riding over.'

Barksdale agreed. 'I tell you,' he said. 'As far as he's concerned, we're both outsiders. Me, because I came late to the cattle trade, even though I know the country. You, because you're an easterner. These people are as clannish as birds. If you ain't got the right kind of feathers, they won't peck with you.'

The girl sighed as they started for home, feeling that she had been completely taken in. In writing him, she had gone far beyond what was proper. He had promised to come, yet with no intention whatever of doing so. Unless—she glanced across the valley with a frown. Unless his horse had fallen with him—they rode such half-broken ponies in this country; and she thought of her brother . . . Well, the ponies were no wilder than the men.

And she knew in that moment that soon she must sell out and go home—defeated, like her brother. Beaten by a country which found the break in you and flooded you with weakness.

CHAPTER TEN

The afternoon before, Chaparro had arrived at Logan's ranch just before sundown. Tom saw him coming and, while he waited for the handyman to ride up, gazed about the ranch yard.

It was a comfortable if modest layout that had been a generation in growing. A nice four-room house of pebbly adobe walls and a sheet-metal roof, standing under a great mesquite tree. There was an ample barn and a long Murphy shed with three walls and a roof, inside which harness and wheeled vehicles were kept. Hills speckled with juniper and brush mounted behind the ranch yard; across the road from the corrals was a long, low ridge with a mound at the end of it. As a boy, Tom used to dig for Indian pots in the mound.

Chaparro stood beside his winter-haired pony with his big *jipi*-straw sombrero held against his stomach. He explained that the rancher was to read the letter and answer it.

Finishing the letter, Logan told Chaparro, 'I'll be there. Six o'clock sharp. How about a drink before you ride back?'

Chaparro thanked him, and they sat on the porch and drank a whiskey. In his dark face, the Mexican's black eyes roved the yard hungrily.

'*Muy bonito*,' he said. 'You understand ranching, *patrón*.'

'Doesn't your boss?'

'He is anxious to learn, perhaps. But when I tell him something, he does not believe it because I am nobody.'

'You ought to get on some land of your own. Then you'd be somebody.'

'*Ay, dios!* But my people—we are the somebodies who are nobody.'

'If I were you—' Logan began, and hesitated. *I'm pretty young to be giving advice*, it occurred to him. And why get Chaparro's hopes up? But he liked the little man even if he did work for a murderer.

Chaparro encouraged him, his eyes keen with pleasure.

'You know where Harshaw is—up in the mountains between this valley and Mexico? There're a dozen dams up there that the miners built years ago and let go to pot when the gravel didn't pan out. There's acres of land they leveled for kitchen gardens and—hell, even townsites. It's good land, a mile deep, and black. I've always thought that if I weren't a rancher, I'd homestead some of that land, rebuild one of the dams, and go to farming.'

Chaparro sipped the whiskey. 'Is possible?'

'Why not? You a resident? It's government land, most of it. And as you made a little money, you could buy up other land. I know of orchards that were planted and are going to rust and fruitborers. Nogales is growing fast—worse luck—and there'll always be a market for anything edible down there.'

Chaparro leaned back. 'Some day—if the *patrón* will give me a day off—'

'Take it,' grinned Logan. 'Hell with the *patrón*. You got time to put in a crop right now! After we get through this Yaqui mess . . . You seen anything over your way?' he asked.

'*Nada*. But I watch. I tell you if I see anything—'

'You do that. I'd sure like to bail out that Julio of mine. He's a good man. And that nephew of his that they've got—only twelve years old. Mind you, I don't blame the Indians. They've been hurt. Hurt by a friend of Barksdale's, and maybe even by your *patrón*. Have another whiskey?'

Shaking his head, Chaparro rose. 'I use the eyes and the ears,' he promised.

'There isn't much time to use anything, but keep me posted.'

The next evening, riding toward the rendezvous at the Monk place, Logan was surprised to see Chaparro loping toward him.

He had been puzzled about the time and place for such a conference, but decided that where the Sutton girl was concerned the unusual was to be expected. It was five o'clock when he saw the man coming.

'Are you all right, Don Tomás?' Chaparro asked, seeming surprised.

'Sure. What's the matter? Have you heard something?'

'No, but why did you not come? I told them you would be there.'

Logan hauled out the big, old silver hunting-case watch of his father's, fat as a baby's fist, and looked at the porcelain face. 'Shoot, it's only five-five! What's all the uproar?'

'But the lady and the *patrón* were there at one!'

Logan shook the watch beside his ear, as though it might somehow be involved in the confusion. 'At *one*? The letter said six.'

Chaparro took off his hat and scratched his black, coarse hair. 'Well, I don' know, Tomás. They wait till after three. Then they go home.'

'Which way'd they go?'

'Well, they go toward the girl's ranch. I don't understand.'

'Neither do I, but let's not get upset about it. You better get back to your wife. Don't leave her alone too much these times. You thought any more about that farming?'

His eyes lighting, Chaparro said: 'We talk all night! I think I homestead. How much it cost itself?'

'Not much. Fifteen dollars, maybe. I'll loan you the money, once this trouble's over. But don't go yon into those mountains till I give you the word.'

'Not in the daytime, even?'

'God, no! The Yaquis are on the prod. You see—if I don't clear things up, I won't be around to help you, either. They'll kill me. They have to set an example by killing everybody that might have been involved. I can't say as I blame them. I wouldn't go back, but I've got to. Thanks, Shorty. Head for home, now.'

Chaparro turned his Spanish pony and rode north toward Barksdale's place. Watching him leave, Logan knew he had a friend there. If anything broke, he'd know about it before long. And what had bought that loyalty? The promise of freedom: the same kind of freedom that had kept the Yaquis fighting for three hundred years.

It was a quarter to six when he reached the Monk place. He circled it carefully and observed the tracks of five or six horses. He found a tin can which had held water, and wondered what that meant. God only knew. God himself probably didn't know why she had summoned him for six and had shown up at one. Looking over the hollow ruin of melting adobe walls, fence-high, he suddenly sniffed.

Tobacco!

Without turning his head, he checked the direction of the wind. At the same moment, his horse flicked its ears and turned its head toward an arroyo cutting through Monk's old orchard.

When Logan set the spurs, the animal

snorted and took off at a hard run. From behind an old galvanized water tank stepped a tall man with a shotgun in his hands. Logan's horse swerved; he brought it to a tuck-under stop and was only twenty feet from the muzzle of the shotgun when the horse, quivering, started to sidle.

'Easy, now,' said Barksdale's man, Hatcher, smiling. 'Thass good right there. I got the damndest collection of junk in the barrel of this gun, it's just shameful.'

Logan heard horses approaching from two directions.

* * *

Barksdale looked him over.

Tom Logan stood against the rusting shell of the water tank, his holster empty, his horse standing some distance away. With Clyde Barksdale had come Joe Breen; from another point, the little twist of rawhide and whiskey smells called Sim Price had ridden in. Breen paced around like a tomcat; he was panting like a man with love on his mind, rather than murder.

'Settle down,' Barksdale growled, finally.

Joe Breen's teeth showed in a grin. 'Man, ain't this sinful?' he chuckled. 'I thought you was the little yellow wolf, Logan. Couldn't nobody Injun up on you.'

'How'd you ever talk the girl into this?'

Logan asked curiously.

'She was all for it.'

'Then where is she?'

He glanced beyond the group lounging before him. It was near dark, now. The lights of a farmhouse down on the Santa Cruz choked him with fear and loneliness. He was not sure what was ahead, but he envied the little Mexican who farmed down there; no one would ever bother him. No one bothered anyone, much, who knuckled down when told to.

'She's leaving it all to me,' said Barksdale. 'I brought a paper along, Logan. Kind of a crude bill of sale, like.'

'On what?'

'Your ranch. It calls for three thousand dollars spread out over a period of five years.'

'That's kind of crude, all right,' Logan agreed.

'You don't want to sell?'

Logan shook his head. 'Hell, no.'

'You're going to tramp around all over Arizona making trouble for people, is that the idea?'

And without any warning, he struck Logan in the mouth with his fist.

Logan's knees buckled and he started to fall. But his rage sustained him, and he lurched up and took a swing at the freighter. The red-faced man called Hatcher shoved the shotgun in his belly, knocking the wind out of him and frightening him half to death. He pressed back against the iron tank. Feinting at his face, Barksdale sank one into his belly. Logan's stomach hardened and the blow did not hurt much.

Pushing Barksdale away, Joe Breen said, 'Hey, back off! Who the hell's party is this?'

Barksdale's piratical grin flashed. 'Thought you'd want him tendered first, Joe,' he said. 'I got the notion somewhere you was toughest with little boys and big girls.'

'You're a comical sonofabitch,' Breen said sourly; and in the same breath he smashed at Logan's face. Logan ducked, and heard Breen wail with pain as his knuckles struck the tank.

Then things got confused.

Barksdale swung at him, Hatcher hit him with the butt of the shotgun, and Price was in with a couple of blows. He was falling. He was not hurt as badly as they thought. They were all so greedy that no one let the other fellow get set for a solid punch. He lay still, until someone kicked him in the rump, and that hurt, and he could not fake unconsciousness any longer. He seized someone's boot as it lashed in at his head, and twisted an ankle viciously.

He was dragged up and once again they were shifting around trying to get a straight shot at him. Logan got in one of his own; Price went out of the fight with a broken jaw. He moaned and held both hands to his face as he staggered away to sit on a wall.

'Hold him! Hold the bastard!' Breen was yelling.

Dazed, Logan felt Barksdale swarm over him from behind, bearing him to his knees, then twisting his arms back and lifting him by them so that he cried out in pain.

'Don't wear yourself out, cowboy,' Barksdale panted. 'This is liable to go on all night.'

Logan's horse was dancing in fright over near the old walls. The whole scene was dim in his mind—dim with dusk and agony, and a raging anger that surmounted everything that was happening to his body.

There was a chiming crash like the stroke of a church bell.

All action halted. They stared up at the top edge of the tank, from which the sound seemed to have come. An instant later a gunshot rolled over the yard from a few hundred feet away.

Slumping against the tank, he watched the men scramble for cover. Then he stumbled across the yard toward his horse. Barksdale's gun roared, and somewhere up the slope he heard the bullet wail off the ground. He got the reins of the horse, and stumbled along a few yards before he found the stirrup and swung up. His head swam, and there was a persistant throb in his shoulders. Like an animal, he looked for cover. First it was the water tank he got behind, then the orchard he was loping through, then the mesquite.

After that he was clear. But he was no longer able to stay on the horse, and when it buck-jumped around a clump of cactus, he floundered from the saddle to the ground. There he lay, hurt and breathless. He was still holding the reins, and the horse halted the moment his weight left its back.

He lay there in the dark, moaning and waiting to be found.

CHAPTER ELEVEN

Late that night, he rode into his ranch yard and slipped from the saddle. He turned the horse into the corral without unsaddling, and shambled to the porch of the house, where he fumbled the door open and went inside. He found a match and lighted a lamp.

From the wall pegs, he took a rifle. While he was loading the gun, he realized he was too far gone to saddle a fresh horse and ride to Barksdale's, as he had planned. And there was a strong vein of practicality in him which robbed him of the enjoyment of a real vendetta; in his heart, he knew he would probably not find Barksdale, would be lucky if he got in the first shot, would more than likely hang if he killed him.

In the end, he left the rifle on the table and stood up. He was practical even to the extent of blowing out the lamp; coal oil was expensive and had to be freighted out here.

He sank onto a big cot made of two-by-four trusses and a couple of hides, and lay there with his arm across his eyes.

He wondered who had fired the shot.

The girl? After helping to set him up for a strike? Had she grown remorseful and come back to try to stop the massacre?

Or was it Shorty—Chapparo—who had taken the great risk, to himself, of standing by to help someone he sensed was a friend?

He thought of his father, ranching this valley in the early days of Apaches and Mexican bandits. It would be a long time before the country tamed down, it seemed. First you had to tame men's hearts: then you tamed the country, encouraged the good range grasses, built railroads, stocked shorthorn cattle which could not be trailed two hundred miles without walking off all their beef. But you didn't do these things overnight.

This country still had a long way to go before it was fit for women and shorthorns.

* * *

He started the next day off at ten o'clock, with a shot of whiskey. Then he went out, squinting at the sunlight. He had a badly swollen jaw and half-closed eyes. He fed his little flock of Rhode Island Red hens, and tossed some alfalfa hay into the corral for the saddle horses. He was surprised to see one of them still wearing a saddle, and, with a groan, he ducked into the corral and unsaddled the animal. To his surprise, it had not taken a roll and broken the tree.

He went into the house and lay down again.

You son of a bitch! he thought. If I don't square with you for trying to turn this county into your private buckpasture. But first Pistola's problems—then his own. True, they were entwined. First, however, the Yaqui gold had to be found and returned. By now it was probably in Kansas City.

Late that afternoon he heard horses whicker, and glanced through the door after picking up his rifle. Two horsemen were riding down from the Indian ridge beyond the wagon road. He studied them an instant, then walked out and sat in a deep rawhide chair with his back against the wall and the rifle across his knees.

The riders came on into the yard. Both were Mexican—tall, straight, appearing in excellent physical condition. Tied behind their saddles were snug little blanket rolls. They wore dark suit pants, collarband shirts buttoned but with no neckties, and leather jackets. Pulling on a Chihuahua bit, one of the riders halted a few yards from the porch and gave Tom Logan a smile. He had keen black eyes, a strong mouth, and a wide black mustache.

‘ ’*Uenas tardes, señor,*’ he said.

‘Hello.’

‘My name is Uranga,’ said the Mexican. ‘I have a cattle ranch in Sonora, near Estación Camargo.’

‘I see.’

‘And this is my *segundo*. May we dismount and refresh our horses?’

‘No. Sorry,’ Logan said. He shook his head.

Urango shrugged and said something in Spanish to his companion, who smiled at the American and nodded understanding. He looked quick, intelligent, and on his toes.

‘*No le hace,*’ said Uranga. ‘I am hoping to buy a small ranch near the border, a place to hold a few hundred cattle from time to time.’

‘Uh-huh,’ Logan said.

‘By any chance, is your ranch for sale?’

Logan shook his head. Both men nodded again, seeming sympathetic with his position, and looked around the ranch yard.

‘Very well,’ said Uranga. ‘You prefer then that we should not water our horses?’

‘That’s right.’

‘Perhaps you too have had trouble with the Indians? A man cannot be too careful. But I assure you, Señor Logan, we are not Yaqui Indians.’

Rising with pain in his ribs, Logan replied: ‘I know that. You’re Rurales. You’re hunting

Yaquis, and if there are any of them around, I don't want them to see you here. I exist by being neutral. By coming here, you not only break my nation's laws, but put me in a dangerous position. Get out.'

'Forgive us. Sometimes your army, too, forgets itself and crosses our frontier. But usually it is to kill countrymen of mine. We are seeking only Indians.'

Logan shook his head. 'My business is cattle. I don't take sides in your wars, and I won't be murdered because someone thinks I do. Who told you I might know something about the Yaquis?'

Uranga's fine black eyes faltered.

'Nacho Ruiz?' Logan pressed him. 'I've seen Sonora "businessmen" in his saloon that walk like Rurales. That's the penalty for spending your life on a horse, my friends. You can't fool a man who spends his life the same way.'

He watched the men swing their horses and ride from the yard. Magnificent horses, panther-like men: nobility itself, among trackers. But even the Rurales, Porfirio Diaz's crack guerrillas and trackers, were not the equal of Yaquis. The Indians had wiped out two armies in the last couple of years, and they were still in business. Perhaps the army's leaders had finally figured out that the only way to stop them was to pinch off the artery that carried their life's blood: supplies.

He felt anger and tension building in

himself, and noisily set the rifle on its wall pegs. Relax, he told himself. You can't fight Barksdale, the Mexican army, and Pistola. Take them one at a time.

The trouble was, they seemed to be coming at him in bunches.

*   *   *

Barksdale took one look at his handyman and knew who had fired the shot that broke up the party.

He had sent Price off to town to get his damned jaw wired up, since he couldn't wag it well enough even to curse, let alone eat. Hatcher had ridden to the ranch house with the freighter, while Breen went back to Miss Sutton's. They slept in the cabin.

In the morning Barksdale walked out on the gallery and bawled: 'Hey, Mex!'

Chaparro came on the gallop, to stand below the railing with one hand at his side and the other trying to make his hair lie flat. His eyes reminded Barksdale of those of a gutshot rabbit waiting to have its head stomped.

'What'd you do after I sent you home yesterday?' he demanded.

'I came back, *patrón*.'

Barksdale sauntered down the steps and stared into his face. 'You ugly little goat! You fired that shot!'

'No! I swear it!'

'Swear what?'

'That I didn't fire that—didn't fire—'

Barksdale grinned. 'What shot you talking about?' he asked.

The handyman looked at the red-faced, smiling Hatcher, looming above him in pants and underwear, and raised and dropped his hands, futilely.

'Saddle the horses,' Barksdale said.

'Como?'

'The horses, stupid. We're going Yaqui hunting.'

Chaparro and his wife begged for mercy and forgiveness. The woman began to wail like a bereaved squaw, and Hatcher slapped her into silence and locked her in the adobe shed where the couple lived. Five minutes later, the three men rode south toward the foothills.

'All I know,' Barksdale told Hatcher, 'is that he's on the wrong team. If we'd 'a' had Logan for another hour, he'd be on his way out today. Who the hell knows what he'll do next?'

Hatcher frowned and struck a match for a black licorice-paper cigarette as they rode. He was ignorant of Barksdale's deal with Breen and, from the freighter's point of view, that was excellent. The faintest smell of guilt on Hatcher would cost him his life today—and Barksdale's as well. They were going into the Yaqui country to try to buy a little friendship. The freighter had not liked some of the questions Pistola had put to him the other night. He wanted to make sure of Pistola's friendship.

Barksdale had only a rough idea of where the Yaquis would be. He did not have to guess their hideout exactly, for up among the mineral-stained ridges there would be many pairs of eyes which would follow his progress into the foothills. His own senses were nearly as sharp. Before long he knew they were being followed.

Halting in some scrub oak below a stony ridge, he spoke to Hatcher. 'Who you reckon them fellows are back there?'

Hatcher twisted to gaze down through the scrub growth. About a half mile behind two horsemen had halted on high ground, pacing after them. Their horses tossed their heads nervously. He started. 'Jesus! You reckon they're Yaquis?'

'On horses? Use your head.'

Hatcher chewed his lip. 'Might be, though, Clyde. The heathens are acting mighty peculiar, from what you tell me.'

Barksdale shook his head. 'Could be a couple of cowboys. Could be Logan. I don't believe it, myself. Nobody but a Mexican keeps a horse nerved up like the animals are back there.'

Hatcher rolled his head around to work out some stiffness left by the evening with Tom Logan. 'Why don't we cut this little greaser loose and head back? Pistola will pick him up anyhow. There's no sense in our tangling with a couple of wandering Mexican bounty hunters.'

'We ain't going to tangle with anybody. We're just riding up to give my friend Pistola a mouse to play with.'

'I don't get you.'

'I mean I want him to know who his friends are. If he ever gets the notion you or I had anything to do with killing his soldiers, it'll be head down over a slow fire for both of us.'

He stepped up their pace, staying below the ridges so that they would be harder to follow. Gradually he became aware that they had entered the Yaqui stronghold. No definite signs told him this. Perhaps it was a lack of signs: the absence of small animals, and of the hawks which preyed on them. A great silence lay over the high foothills, with only the whisper of wind through the thready spines of Spanish bayonet. They followed a canyon with raw banks cut back by torrents, until it brought them to a small rincon a half-mile across, hemmed in by wooded hills. A few dozen cattle grazing here raised their heads to stare. Near the center of the bowl there was a great, jagged stump on the bank of a gully, its dead white trunk sprawled beside it. Barksdale discerned a gleam of lighter wood where a small branch had been broken off for fuel. The stump somehow resembled a sacrificial altar.

Chaparro, sensing that they had reached a

critical point in their journey, began to argue. He was through with pleading, and now he began saying things he had heard from someone else.

'The Yaquis will kill you, as you intend to let them kill me,' he said, his eyes glittering. 'You are probably a *llori*-lover. You are trying to buy their friendship. Who knows? Maybe you yourself killed those men!'

Barksdale laughed. 'Listen who's talking—a *llori*!'

'No—we peasants are not *llori*. The *llori* have money for shoes.'

Barksdale kicked Chaparro's horse with his boot, and they rode on to the twisted white stump with its rotten heart. He spoke to Hatcher, who held a gun on the Mexican while Barksdale slipped to the ground, collectd some pitch-wood from a burn on the tree-trunk, and built a small fire. After it was blazing well, he scraped up damp leaves and all but extinguished the fire. A sweetish white smoke spiraled into the air.

In a few minutes they heard the flat thump of a drum.

The cattle raised their heads again, though the Indians were not yet visible. When they arrived, they came trotting in from all sides, perhaps two dozen of them, as Barksdale had expected. He saw Pistola—stocky and raisin-brown, with, a greasy red headband setting off his black hair. The chief jumped from the gully and came toward them.

Before Barksdale could explain what had brought them, Chaparro commented babbling his own explanation. Barksdale's fist collided, with his ear and he sprawled from the saddle. Several Indians ringed him as he huddled on the ground.

'He was working for me,' Barksdale growled. 'I knew he'd been prowling around at night. Last night I caught him coming in. He admitted he'd been out bounty hunting for Yaquis.'

Chaparro sat up. 'It is not true! I went to—to warn Don Tomás Logan. Then I—'

Barksdale's grin split his dark face. 'So that was it. The two of you, eh? And maybe you were selling information to them fellers following us.'

Pistola spoke a few words of Yaqui, and the Indians dragged Chaparro up. With Barksdale's rope, they lashed him to the tree stump.

'They are Rurales,' Pistola said. 'How long have they been around?'

'Never seen them before.'

'Nor will you see them again.'

Barksdale glanced at Hatcher, who was staring bug-eyed at the Indians. There was nothing particularly alarming in their appearance—baggy peasant pants, collarband shirts, and neckerchiefs at their throats—nor was it the rifles they carried that made them seem so sinister. It was their faces: the look of hawks in their eyes. Like hawks in a cage you wouldn't think of offering a morsel, knowing they would take the finger as well. Disdainful and independent.

On a hillside, a drum thumped three times.

Pistola gestured. 'Into the trees,' he said.

At a jog, the men rode to the nearest cover and dismounted. Two Yaquis took the reins of their mounts and led them further into the brush, as Hatcher and Barksdale crouched behind a log to watch. The bowl was empty now. With his face turned up, Chaparro stood tied to the stump, praying loud.

The Rurales suddenly appeared from the wash only a hundred yards from the stump. With great prudence, they studied the scene. No doubt, Barksdale conjectured, it was the presence of the cattle which satisfied them that they were safe.

They rode forward to find out why the Mexican had been left for the buzzards and the ants.

Some of the cattle, grazing near the edges of the rincon, began drifting across the bare ground toward the stump.

CHAPTER TWELVE

'Why did they leave you here? Why should we release you, if you will not answer a simple question?'

Chaparro continued to pray, moving his lips in a whisper, while the Rural, Uranga, stood before him with his fists on his hips.

'Did you betray them in something? What were the men's names?'

The other Rural raised his rifle to point at the hillside. 'There's a beef carcass up there,' he said. 'But there are no buzzards.'

Uranga nodded 'The men we were following frightened away the buzzards. We're looking for Indians, don't you understand?' He said intently, leaning from the hips toward Chaparro. 'The kind who slaughter little men like you.'

At last Chaparro's gaze dropped from the water-clear sky to the hard-fleshed brown face of the tracker. 'And like you,' he said.

Taken aback, Uranga straightened. With his well-booted feet planted in the earth, he peered around the little arena-like bowl. The grazing cattle, which had inspired his confidence in the beginning, continued to graze peacefully on the tender early-summer grass. Several had come quite close, and he tried to see a brand, but the marks were still obscured by long winter hair.

'All right—like me, too,' he shrugged. 'But if we capture them, put chains on them and ship them to Valle Nacional to work in the chicle forests, then they bother no one, eh? That is why we look for them. Are you an American citizen?'

'I think so. My father was a citizen, though I was raised in Magdalena. I do not think it matters much.'

'Why not?'

'Because of the Indians.'

'What Indians?' asked the other tracker, quickly.

Chaparro closed his eyes. Uranga took a step toward him and smashed his palm across the prisoner's mouth. 'What Indians?' he shouted.

Among the trees a drum thudded with a hard wooden resonance, another echoed it, then another, and all at once the air throbbed with a barbarious rhythm. Both Rurales turned to run for their horses, standing only yards away. But the steers blocked their way. And from behind each steer rose an Indian who had ridden it from the trees; clinging to its side. A few shots exploded; both horses fell, and the shorter Mexican, who carried his rifle, stumbled and went down. The tall man, Uranga, attempted to draw his revolver, but the Yaquis sprang on him and crushed him to the earth.

Behind the log, Barksdale and Hatcher looked at each other.

'Goddamn,' Barksdale muttered. 'Wish they'd shot the bastard. Oh, hell. Maybe he'll die quick.'

But the man died slowly, taking the better part of an hour to bleed and scream his life out. For Pistola knew him, and pronounced a more severe sentence than death. It was turnabout. Yaquis who were caught were first tortured for information. Then, if they survived, they were sold to labor contractors for seventy-five dollars a head, to be used in the jungles of southern Mexico.

Before it was over, Clyde Barksdale knew one thing for sure: he was ready to take his profit and settle down to being careful for a few years. Tonight, or tomorrow, he must catch up with Joe Breen and arrange for the split. He saw no fun in running around inside a circle of Indians armed with machetes, with his guts dragging in the dirt.

But he was grinning when Pistola sought him after the torture. 'They were *lloris*, all right,' he chuckled.

'Were they the ones who killed the kin?' asked the chief.

'Quién Sabe?' replied Barksdale, Careful neither to step into the trap by a too-enthusiastic affirmation, nor to back from it suspiciously by exaggerated doubt. 'Maybe they're your killers. They're sure as hell off the reservation. But you'd think they'd 'a' took off sooner than this, wouldn't you?'

Pistola's obsidian eyes left his face and turned to the Mexican, still tied to the stump awaiting his turn. Again he looked into Barksdale's face, at greater length this time. Finally he said:

'I will keep the man until Tomás Logan comes again. Say nothing to him. Perhaps this one will talk before Don Tomás comes with more lies.'

*   *   *

It was near dusk when the men reached the valley. Barksdale was anxious to talk to Joe Breen, but it was important not to let Hatcher have a look at his cards.

'You'd better get back to your work,' he told him. 'Pistola won't bother us any. Keep working, and don't give anybody the idea you feel guilty about anything.'

Hatcher looked puzzled. 'I don't. Why should I?'

'You shouldn't, by God, or you're a dead cowboy. But looking down the blade of a machete like we done today is apt to make a man feel guilty even if he ain't. Let a Yaqui smell fear on you, and you're done. Is that branding corral about finished?'

Hatcher looked at his callused palms. 'Yep. And so am I. I get pains in my shoulders every time I roll a cigarette. There is more rocks in this ground than there is tombstones in the Nogales graveyard.'

Barksdale laughed, slapped him on the back, and rode off toward his ranch house three miles away. Ten minutes later he turned west toward Laura Sutton's. Riding in, he was careful to keep behind a hill so that he would not be seen. He entered the lower end of the horse trap and rode to within a few rods of the bunkhouse before dismounting.

Like all such mouse- and dust-ridden bachelor homes, the long room smelled of liniment. There were a dozen cots, only one of which was occupied. Breen lay on it, smoking, as Barksdale entered. Dusk had gathered like cobwebs in the chilly adobe building. No lamp burned.

'What you up to?' Barksdale asked, then saw the gun in Breen's hand. 'Hey, for the love of—!'

Breen, lying on his elbow, pouched the gun. 'Heard you coming. Why didn't you give me a hail? Man could get himself killed thataway.'

Barksdale's weight made the cot beside Breen's creak. 'We've got to make some plans, Joe,' he said.

Breen listened to the story about the Rurales and Chaparro. 'I reckon we'd *better* plan,' he agreed. 'Got anything in mind?'

'The sooner we make the split, the better. If I was you, I'd put my share in a valise and take the train to Bisbee. I'd go too, but if I went I couldn't ever come back.'

'Neither could I,' said Breen.

'Do you want to cone back?'

Breen stirred, scowling. Barksdale squinted at his bony face with its long planes and knobs.

'Not particularly. But there's a couple of other places I can't go back to either. Man could run out of space.'

'All right—stay here. But don't start spending money. If you want to spend money, go somewhere else to do it.'

'What about you?'

'I ain't going to change one thing about my life. Not for a year. Then I take a cattle-buying trip to Denver between seasons. I open a checking account with half my money. I come back through Albuquerque and open another. After I get back, I put drafts through for cash when I need any.'

Breen sighed: 'I ain't got that kind of patience, Clyde. I want money, and I want it now.'

'Then you'd better take yours and clear out. Nobody'll suspect you anyhow. Lot of other people will be taking off, if Pistola hangs around much longer.'

'. . . When?' Breen asked, after a moment.

'Two, three days. When it's time, we'll ride over to the cache and make the cut. I'll leave my share in the mine tunnel.'

He stood up. 'Okay?'

'I reckon that's the best way.'

Barksdale's big hand went out in the darkness, and Breen reached up and gripped it.

At the door, Barksdale said: 'What's the girl up to?'

'This will kill you,' Breen said. 'She's reading back issues of the *Livestock Journal*! This morning she asked me what I thought about seeding some of the overgrazed spots with timothy. I thought Timothy was one of the twelve apostles. And she wrote a letter to Logan, asking if there was something wrong. Then she tore it up.'

'If she ever forgets to tear one up,' said Barksdale, 'see that *you* don't.'

* * *

Breen waited until his hoof sounds had faded, then strode to the door and stared after him. Certain that he had left, the foreman walked around to the kitchen door and rapped. The *galopina*, a little Mexican girl about twelve, came at his knock. *'Mánde?'*

'Tell the señorita I want to see her.'

'Mánde?' the girl repeated.

Breen, with an almost complete lack of Spanish, said impatiently: 'The lady! The señorita—'

'What is it, Joe?' Laura's voice called. From another door, she entered the lamplit kitchen.

Breen removed his hat. 'I forgot to order salt block when I was in town, Miss Laura. I reckon I'd better ride in.'

'Tonight?' The girl stared at him.

'I don't mind,' Breen said.

'I'm sure it would keep, Joe,' Laura said.

Breen frowned at the mud-scraper beside the stoop. 'I don't mind riding in. Besides, I want to talk to Marshal Duffy. See how things are coming.'

The girl shrugged. 'Whatever you say.'

He nodded. 'Thanks. Anything I can get for you?'

'Hardly. All the stores will be closed.'

'Oh, yeah.' Breen grinned. 'You know how it is when the feeling's on you. You can't get it off you till you do a thing.'

'I really don't know, but enjoy yourself, and don't come home drunk.'

'No, ma'am.'

Ma'am! Walking away, the gunman wrinkled his nose. This job is rotting my brains, he thought. He hadn't called a girl *ma'am* since he was in school. He felt a hot, pulsating urge to straighten her out on this business of who gave the orders.

CHAPTER THIRTEEN

From the hills above Nogales, Breen looked down on the lighted business district and a sprinkling of street lamps. In the thin desert air, each light had the clean, hard glitter of a star. It was ten o'clock. He started down the flinty road into the big border village, hungry for a woman and thirsty for whiskey. And another appetite gnawed at him which only settling with Logan would ever appease.

But the first thing was to tell Nacho that Barksdale was getting restless. Nacho still had that knife at his throat, and without any question he would just as soon start cutting as not.

The gunman stabled his horse, preferring not to leave it in front of the saloon like a calling card. In this kind of game, the less you told other men about yourself, the better.

In Nacho Ruiz's International Saloon, there was a blue fog of tobacco smoke, a fine heady fragrance of every kind of liquor a man could name, and a shrill idiotic chorus of girls' voices bleating from the little stage at the end of the hall. A half-dozen girls were loping around in net stockings, short skirts and spangled bodies, singing as they danced. Breen grinned and took a deep breath. He decided to put off talking to Nacho tonight and catch him in the morning.

At a table near the stage he saw an empty chair. He pulled it around for a better view of the girls. Settling himself, he looked for a waiter. But at that moment a man in a dapper brown suit moved in beside him.

'You like the girls, señor?' he asked.

Breen's glance tilted up. It was Nacho, dressed to the eyes, highlights of perspiration on his small, fat nose, shaped like a parrot's beak. Breen began rolling a cigarette.

'Where'd you find them beasts, Nacho?' he asked.

'It's a little dramatic troupe that got stranded in Tucson. I had an opportunity to help them out for a couple of weeks.'

'I might be able to help the one in the green skirt a little myself, if I had the opportunity.'

Nacho patted his shoulder. 'I'll fix it up, Joey. After we talk. Come up to my room in a half hour.'

He moved away without waiting to hear Breen's ideas on mixing women and business.

Later, waiting in the saloonkeeper's private room, Breen sat on a green plush chair as soft as a woman's lap. The room was thick with odors of shaving lotions and dark leaf tobacco. The room was half-woman, half-man, hung with those depressing drapes which made him think of a funeral parlor.

The door opened and Nacho entered briskly, closed it, and sat on the edge of another chair, his manner forceful and commanding.

'We gotta close this up,' he said curtly. 'There was two Rurales in town yesterday. Not in uniform, but I knew them. Things are getting touchy when we have two lawmen, a couple of Rurales, and half the ranchers in the country beginning to mix in it.'

'You don't need to worry about the Rurales any more,' Breen said. 'They're dead. Barksdale done for them.'

Nacho's brows went up. 'How was this?'

Breen recounted the story. 'Did you sic them on Logan?' he asked. 'Seems like they'd been out thataway.'

'I didn't hear the question,' Nacho smiled. 'But here's my answer: let's wrap everything up and split the blanket.'

'Tonight? Tomorrow? Say the word.'

'Pretty soon.' The saloonkeeper went to a marble topped washstand, poured water and rinsed his hands. Breen was always fascinated by the things he did. Nacho had this urge to keep clean—clean suits, fresh shirts three times a day. Maybe he had just touched a woman, and now he was licking himself like a cat.

As he dried his hands on a huck-towel, Nacho said: 'Sure, I sent the Rurales out there. That may have helped us a little. But Pistola drags deep, he looks a gift horse over like it had a fuse coming out of its ear. There's only one sure way to get clean, and that's to give him a man with bloody hands.'

Breen shifted on the chair, troubled. He sensed a new complication coming.

'You were talking about Logan last time you were in,' Nacho recalled. 'Thought anymore about him?'

Breen winked. 'I didn't hear the question. He's got some welts on his face, but I don't know nothing about them.'

'And that little squirrel-faced swamper of Clyde Barksdale's has got his jaws wired together. But you don't know nothing about that either, I suppose. Well, I'll tell you something, Joey. Logan's young, but he's smart, and when you men took him on the other night, you told him for sure what he's been trying to find out: that you're the ones he's after.'

Breen wiped his mouth, scowling. 'It was Clyde's idea.'

'All right. This is mine. You're going to dig up part of the money—say five hundred dollars—and bury it under Logan's fireplace. While you're doing that, I'm leaving a note for Pistola at a certain spot. It will say, "Look under Logan's fireplace. He got drunk and told a girl." Something like that. Then we split up. Bring my share of the money to town and maybe I take off on a little trip. You put yours on a pack horse and head out. It don't matter where, nobody's going to follow you now.'

'Except Clyde,' said Breen.

'Hell, can't you handle Clyde?' the saloonkeeper sneered. 'Clyde is a pig's bladder full of wind. Stick a knife in him: he'll whistle and collapse. He won't follow you, but if he does that's the way to handle him.'

Suddenly Joe Breen felt a weight slide from his back. He realized he had carried it for days, but now he felt physically better; sitting up straight on the chair, he knew his worries had been bearing down like a knapsack full of horseshoes. Now it was almost over. A shiver of delight went over him as he thought of Logan watching the Yaquis dig under his fireplace . . .

'You're okay, Nacho,' he said. 'You may have a nose like a greased banana, but you've got a mind like a rattlesnake. When do we move?'

Nacho laughed, but his bulging brown eyes did not take part in the fun. 'We'll go out tonight and split it up. I'll bring my share in after I leave the note. You can pick yours up whenever you feel like it. I'll fix things downstairs and we can take off.'

*   *   *

Tom Logan felt better.

It was midafternoon. He had loafed around the ranch house all day yesterday after the Rurales left, but this morning he had ridden up to one of his line camps. Here he had cutting corrals and a squeeze-chute for branding. Getting on and off a horse was still an act of heroism. There were bruised muscles in his thighs, pummelled by the boots of Barksdale's crowd, with all the agony potential of a carbuncle on the neck. Riding along tight-mouthed with discomfort, he checked the cows in his herd. A few calves were yet to be dropped, but most of the crop was ready for tallying. Ready for branding, castrating, and other things, too, but the entire work of the ranch was stalled.

Since yesterday he had been plotting a party for Joe Breen.

It might be the only way to crack this melon and see what was hidden inside it. Yet it might also be the quickest way to get himself killed. He was going to trap Joe Breen like a coyote and haul him up to Pistola's camp. He would-explain about Breen's spending the Spanish coin. He would try to implicate Barksdale, too, but for the time being he dared not include the freighter in his party. There was a suspicion in Logan's mind that Barksdale might know the Yaquis from his old days in the freight trade.

Go easy there, something told him.

Reaching his home place in the dusk, he rode up to the corral and swung down. The horse turned its head toward the cabin; with a startled stroke of his heart, Logan sprawled on the ground. He yanked his Colt, almost dropped. it, cocked the gun and studied the ground to see what had attracted the horse's attention.

He heard an animal-like wail from the porch. With the muscles of his ears tightening, he waited. Someone came down the steps and into view: a woman. She was hurrying toward the corral, sobbing as she came.

Raising himself on his elbows, he studied her. He hoped at first that it was Laura Sutton, but this woman had black hair in long braids coming forward over her shoulders, and she was very small. Except for her slightness, she resembled a squaw. After a moment he knew her.

It was the wife of Chaparro.

With a groan, he got to his fee and holstered his gun. The woman ran up, falling to her knees when she reached him and seizing his hand.

'Mi marido—mi esposo—Se fué!'

A flash of cold went over Logan. 'What happened to him?'

'The *patrón* took him away yesterday. He locked me in the shed. I broke the door last night. All day I have been walking, looking for my husband.'

'He's not here, Manuela,' Logan said. 'Where did they take him?'

She was not sure; there had been talk about the Yaquis.

'Oh, God!' Logan groaned. Immediately he

wished he could take the exclamation back, for it told her he knew the matter was serious. She began wailing again. He pulled her to her feet and shook her.

'Now, stop this. They won't hurt him. They're pretty good people. They may hold him a few days. I'll look for him tomorrow—'

'But tomorrow he will certainly be dead!'

'We'll have something to eat, and then I'll tell you what I may be able to do.'

He finished tending the horse as she stood by. In the ranch house, he lighted a lamp and set it on the kitchen table. As he was stuffing pitch-splinters into the woodstove, he noticed that there had been a small fire in the fireplace while he was gone.

The girl was slicing bacon at the sink. 'Manuela,' he said, 'did you build a fire while you waited for me?'

She looked at him, then at the little stone fireplace tucked into the corner by the parlor door. 'No, certainly not, señor. I did not come in. I would not do such a thing.'

'Somebody did. I thought maybe you made some coffee.'

He finished stoking the fire, lighted it, and went to inspect the fireplace. By God, someone had been here and built a fire! He went to one knee and brushed some of the coals aside. There was still a trace of warmth on the hearth.

He peered into the pantry to see what food,

if any, was missing. It was quite possible that a couple of Yaqui soldiers, or those Rurales, had been here and helped themselves to some food. But nothing was missing.

'I've got to turn the horses into the trap,' he told the girl.

Walking out, he lifted a rifle from the rack by the door.

It was too dark to see much. The last rusty-green light sprayed across the sky, but the ragged hills were lost in night. Quietly he moved about, glancing into the barn, studying the hillsides behind the cabin, the old Indian mound before it. Before returning to the house, he placed a ladder against the parapet roof. From a lean-to where he stored odds and ends, he carried blankets and a bull's-eye lantern to the ladder. He carried them to the flat, asphaltic roof.

Returning, he found the simple dinner of bacon, eggs, and fried grits ready. Chaparro's wife carried his plate to the table and returned to stand by the stove. Logan waved his hand.

'Sit down and eat,' he said. 'I'm not used to servants.'

'And I am not used to sitting down with the *gente*,' said the girl, almost primly. But she brought a plate of food and ate, sitting nervously on the edge of her chair.

Logan was tuned like a fiddle string to every sound. He ate with a frown, pretending not to be concerned. He talked of the possibility of

Chaparro's homesteading in the hills.

'Don't see why he couldn't make a go of it. He's a good worker. I've got an old fresno he can use to rebuild one of those dams.'

While she washed the dishes, he collected some food in a fifty-pound sugar sack and carried it outside. He moved the food, two rifles and some ammunition to the roof and came back. The girl was still cleaning the kitchen He knew she was distressed by the patina of grease and smoke over everything.

'Let it go,' he said. 'Some day I'll get a cook, or a wife, and you'll never know the place.'

'I might as well be working,' the girl said.

'Manuela, I think we'd better go up on the roof for the night. I'm not afraid of the Yaquis, but I've got other enemies these days.' Holding a dish towel, she stared at him, the pupils of her eyes enormous. 'Your husband probably saved my life, and I'm going to do what I can to save his. In the meantime, I'll take care of his wife the best way I can. Let's go.'

He led her from the cabin, leaving a lamp burning in the kitchen. She climbed the ladder and he went up after her.

'Tomorrow I'll go looking for Chaparro,' he said. 'If I went tonight, I'd get shot before my friends recognized me.'

He pulled the ladder up and laid it alongside the parapet. Enough leaves had collected on the roof so that he was able to scrape up a little pallet for the girl in one corner, and another for himself at the other end of the house.

'Whatever you hear,' he said, 'don't make a sound. I'll be hearing it too, and I'll do what's to be done. All right?' He smiled.

She nodded. *'Si, señor.'*

He had picked a spot at the side of the house near the corral, so that, should he doze off, the sound of the horses would wake him if anyone came around. He dozed off immediately, and did not wake until the girl squeezed his shoulder.

'Excuse me, señor. You said you would leave at daylight.'

He groaned, cleared his throat, and muttered: 'Thanks.' She hurried off to her end of the house as he sat up, scrubbing his face with his palms. Coming fully awake, he crouched at the parapet's edge and gazed about the hillsides. A mighty twittering of birds filled the morning; the sun was still a promise behind the hills. He heard a cardinal's woody song. In the corral the horses were gazing at the house.

He made ready to travel. After he had lowered the ladder, he told Manuela:

'Pull the ladder up after I reach the ground. Nobody knows you're here, so if you keep out of sight they won't think to look for you on the roof. When I come back, I'll have your *esposo* with me. Don't worry.'

In reply, the girl began to sob again,

covering her face with her hands. Logan felt rather gloomy himself, knowing the Yaqui predilection for mischief with knives, ants, and cactus whips.

He saddled his strongest traveling horse, hoping it might be carrying double when he returned, and left just as the edge of sun appeared above the hills.

CHAPTER FOURTEEN

About three miles west of the spot where Julio had been captured, a small meadow was tucked into a cleft of the mountains. Almost centered in the meadow was a jagged white stump near the bank of a gully. For as long as he could remember, the stump had done duty as a mailbox. When there was something Tom's father wanted the Yaquis to know—that he needed a temporary laborer, that there had been suspicious-looking Mexicans around—he would leave a note in this stump. Before long his need would be filled, or some token of response would be found in the stump.

It was also the best place he knew to find a Yaqui.

It was after ten, the morning hot and redolent of pitch, when he rode up the meadow. Once he heard a sound behind him; he glanced back but saw nothing. Yet he knew the pucker-string of the trap was being pulled tight.

Nearing the stump, he saw a swarm of blowflies crawling over some stains on the ground. His stomach squeezed as he remembered the graves he had blundered onto before . . . He could hear the flies humming, like bees swarming in a tree. Glancing around, he saw several grisly-looking bits of flesh on the ground, crawling with maggots.

Oh, my God, he thought. *They've already finished him.*

And he was furious. Underdogs or not—Goddamn it, they had some responsibility to the human race! Pistola ought to be able to tell a liar from a saint better than that.

* * *

He dismounted and looked for other signs of what had happened. It was possible the Rurales had blundered in and had been butchered. Anything was possible. But what was probably true was that Barksdale had turned Chaparro over to the Indians for torture.

He raised his revolver and fired a single shot. Then he walked to the stump, removed the two-foot length of false branch which served as a plug for the hole where messages were left, and peered inside. It was empty.

He heard the Indians coming, trotting

quietly over the loose earth. He leaned against the stump and waited for them to gather around him. They came quietly, a dozen of them, with Luis Muñoz, called Pistola, confronting him with narrow, suspicious eyes.

'What did you do with the Mexican?' Logan demanded.

Pistola's brown features hardened. 'You know what we do with all Mexicans.'

'If you've killed him, you've sinned worse than the Mexicans have sinned against you. You've caught the murder sickness from them.'

'What Mexican do you mean?'

'Barksdale's man.'

Pistola came toward him. He took the Colt from Logan's holster. 'I thought perhaps you meant the Rurales you sent to spy on us.'

'I didn't send them. Someone sent them to me. I told them to leave without watering their horses.'

* * *

Lifting his shoulders, the Yaqui smiled. 'It's all right. I would have thanked you. They left us without watering their horses, too . . .'

Shocked, Logan looked at the stains on the ground. 'Was that—?'

Pistola nodded. 'The other man is alive. For a little longer. We have stayed too long already. A place acquires a smell when soldiers stay too long, and the wolves come. Soon we kill the hostages and leave. You have had much time and have learned nothing.'

'I've learned a lot. Look at my face! I've learned not to trust Clyde Barksdale or the Sutton woman. Also I know who has some of your gold. Joe Breen, who works for Miss Sutton, spent one of the gold pieces two weeks ago.'

'Why didn't you tell me this before?'

'I wanted to find Breen first, but Breen and Barksdale found me before I found him. They'd have beaten me to death if that man you're holding hadn't scared them off.'

Pistola frowned. 'So the man Breen has the gold.'

'At least part of it. I don't know much about Barksdale, but he's tried to block me from the start. I think the two of them killed your men and hid the money. Who else but a man like Barksdale could have walked up as a friend and then killed them?'

'Or a man like you?'

'Like me—but I didn't do it.'

'Will you prove it to us?' Pistola asked.

Suddenly and definitely, Logan knew something was up: the whole conversation had led toward it.

'I've been trying to prove it,' he said. 'What do you mean?'

Pistola pulled a fold of paper from the pocket of his shirt. He handed it to Logan, who opened it and read a dozen-odd words written Spanish in violet ink.

Under Logan's kitchen fireplace. A girl he talked to told me.

*   *   *

He felt his face flame. His hand clenched the paper. 'This is Ruiz's handwriting! I've seen it. You believe a man like Nacho Ruiz, a whoremonger—but you won't believe me!'

'We believe our friends. You have been our friend. This man has been our friend, too. I don't say that it was Ruiz. But this man has helped us many times, and this is the note we found here.'

Logan knew now why a fire had been built in the kitchen; he could guess what they would find under the scorched mud-bricks. He put the note in his pocket. Pistola saw it, but did not comment.

'Why haven't you looked in my cabin?' Logan asked.

'Because it might be a trap.'

'So you'll kill me without looking?'

'No. Four men will go with you. If nothing is found, perhaps it will mean that this other man is no longer to be trusted.'

'Oh, you'll find something all right,' Logan said. 'Someone built a fire yesterday while I was away. He was covering the marks of his digging. Let me tell you what you'll find: just enough of your money to make it look as if I'd been hiding it, a little bit here, a little bit there. But not enough to matter much to the ones who have the rest.'

'That may be,' the Yaqui said. 'They will take you now and bring you back if they find anything.'

He spoke to several of his men. Logan caught a few words. Surprisingly, most of what the general was saying had to do with the Lord and the Most Holy Mother. He seemed to be exhorting them to a sort of holy war against the forces arrayed against the kin. It was small comfort to Logan.

Riding bareback, four Yaquis came from the trees at Pistola's signal. With two warriors leading and two following, the party started for the ranch.

CHAPTER FIFTEEN

That morning Barksdale had killed one of Manuela's chickens and put it to stew in a Dutch oven. He was morosely uneasy, nettled by a sense of increasing danger. During the morning he had quartered the area trying to pick up the woman's trail, but was unsuccessful. He was not unduly worried about her: she knew little or nothing about his affairs, and even if she blundered into the Yaqui camp she couldn't tell them anything before they finished her off. His expectation was that she would find the trail he and Hatcher and Chaparro had left yesterday and follow it into the mountains.

Then—adiós Manuela. Indians could have more fun with a captive female than a kid with a barrel of hard candy.

The chicken was only half-cooked when he ate it. The meat clung to the bone, and he tore it off impatiently, staring from the gallery of his place down across the valley. Thinking about Breen. Worrying over Pistola. The Yaqui general was nobody's simpleton, and he had a lot of time to think up there in the hills.

One of the things he must be thinking about was where Joe Breen was when his men were killed. He knew Breen was out of town. But he also knew the timing was close enough that the man could have participated in the ambush before leaving.

* * *

Barksdale threw a drumstick over the railing, leaned back, and had a pull from a bottle of Mexican wine. Drawing up his lower lip, he reflected. Maybe this very suspiciousness of Pistola's could be put to use.

If Breen took off suddenly, Pistola might decide that was proof enough: Breen was the killer and thief. Chances were he could never do anything about it, but it would pull his attention from other people, such as Clyde Barksdale.

If he got suspicious too soon, however, captured Breen, and did a thorough job of questioning him, Breen would begin chattering like a magpie.

Barksdale's pulse quickened. He pushed his plate aside and rose. Time had been running out, and he had not been aware of it. Great God! Breen was a stick of blasting powder with a short fuse, and he had left him free to roam!

Barksdale threw a saddle on a horse and rode from the yard.

* * *

Keeping to the gullies and behind rocky hills, he made his way to the Sutton place with the same care he used to employ in Sonora when the snakes were out.

Laura Sutton was in the yard when he arrived; the buggy was hitched and she was depositing articles behind the seat. One was a cardboard box, and from the great care with which she held it upright, he would take an oath it was a cake.

The sun burnished the soft waves of Laura's hair and found warm tones in her skin. She wore a light summer dress which reminded him that she was all woman, and put him in mind of the fact that there was other business to get on with once things settled down.

‘Where to?’ he asked amiably.

For a moment her gaze evaded his. Then she looked at him frankly. ‘I’m driving over to Tom Logan’s, Clyde.’

Barksdale raised his brows. He dismounted. With a hard palm, he rubbed dust from the side-rail of the buggy. ‘Always did hear tell,’ he said, ‘that some women go after punishment like it was candy.’

Laura gave her head an impatient toss. ‘That isn’t true, Clyde, and I don’t like it. Whatever else he may be, he’s a neighbor. And I’m worried about him.’

Barksdale pinched her cheek. ‘You’re beginning to talk like an Arizonan, Miss Laura. But you still think like an easterner. What could *you* do to help Logan, if he did have troubles?’

Laura raised her shoulders. ‘He might be hurt! Use your imagination. I’m going to find out.’

‘Excuse me. All you’re going to find out is that being a woman is no protection in Indian country. I’ve seen the bodies of women the Yaquis—’ He broke off, frowning.

She turned her face away. ‘Clyde,’ she said, in reproof.

‘I’m sorry. But this thing has heated up faster than I expected. There was two Mexicans murdered yesterday not ten miles from here.’

‘Murdered!’

'I came across their bodies. Don't know who they were, but I gave them a decent burial. I never saw deader men in my life—and it wasn't no white men killed them. You expect this sort of thing in Sonora. But up here—'

* * *

The girl hugged herself, staring across the valley. 'Perhaps it was a band of Yaqui soldiers—I mean, they may have thought they were in Mexico—'

Barksdale took her shoulders and made her look at him. Big and solemn, he gazed into her eyes. 'Face it, Laura. The Yaquis know that border better than we do. Tomorrow I'm going to move you to town.'

He saw her eyes rove in the direction of Logan's ranch. After a moment she said, 'Will you promise to ride over and talk to him if I agree?'

'Sure I will,' said Barksdale.

'All right.'

The freighter squeezed her shoulders, savoring the slenderness of them. Then he glanced at the bunkhouse. 'I'll look in on your foreman before I take off.'

'I don't believe Joe is here,' Laura said. 'I asked him to look over my Flat Rock pasture. It's so overgrazed I'm thinking of seeding it with timothy or brome. He hasn't come back yet.'

'When'd he leave?'

'Early this morning.'

'Flat Rock's only a half-hour's ride.'

'He's probably looking over the calf herd, too.'

'More'n likely,' Barksdale said drily.

Something he had tried not to think about struck him like a stone between the eyes. Breen—the stupid, greedy gun-tramp!—may have dug up that money again, moved it bit by bit, and taken off with it!

'I'll check on him,' he said calmly.

In a clammy fear, he started for Laura's Flat Rock pasture, some hilly sections of grazing land under a perpendicular scarp, famed particularly for rocks and locoweed. There was no evidence of Breen's having so much as visited the branding corrals or the dirt water tank.

Barksdale's mouth set. An hour from here, halfway up the steep foothills, were some manmade coyote holes where a few dozen forgotten miners had done their fruitless assessment work, given up, and left behind color-streaked mounds of rock and rusting narrow-gage rails. In one of those tunnels, he and Breen had hidden Pistola's ten thousand dollars.

Barksdale slashed his horse with the end of his catchrope. The animal snorted and dug out.

Never forgetting that he was in enemy

country, he switch-backed up the scarps to the mining area. Near the mine he dismounted, hid his horse in some junipers, and planted himself in a wedge of rocks overlooking the foothills. Farsighted from years of such scrutiny, he could see a jackrabbit farther than most men could follow a deer. Convinced that no one was following him, he slipped back and led the horse to the mine. Leaving it ground-tied, he moved quickly into the tunnel.

Like most old mines, it smelled of wet earth and rodents. But rats and mine water had never hurt gold. Only rats like Breen.

You sonofabitch! he choked, if you've been into that money—!

He paced along the rotting ties of the tiny railway. The tunnel took a bend and the light was gone. The darkness pressed like moth's wings against his face. He struck a match and groped on. They had left a candle within six feet of the treasure. He searched for it, found its waxy residue on a rock, and had to swallow fear like a chunk of half-chewed beef.

Someone had been here since they had buried the gold. Two inches of candle he had left were gone. His mouth dry, he pried a few splinters from, a rotting stull and lighted them.

In the sickish light of the tiny torch, he saw a small excavation between the tracks.

* * *

Barksdale rolled two cigarettes and smoked them.

If I was his size, and stupid, where would I go? he asked himself.

Quit fooling yourself, he thought. He's stupid like an Apache witch doctor. He only made you think he was stupid. But all the time he was moving that gold. Now it's gone, and he's hopped the train to Bisbee after it. Perhaps he had shipped it to some other town and gone to join it—his golden bride, the gold-plated whore he would romance wildly for two weeks before finishing with a foolish grin and a headache as wide as Texas.

Oh, you cheating yellow dog!

The things I could have done with that money. The land I was going to buy, the shorthorn cattle. You know something, Joe? he thought ironically. I was going to leave *you* in that hole! Enlarge it a bit, maybe. Pile some rocks over your chicken-skinned carcass. But your share was always going to be a piece of lead no bigger than the tip of your little finger. I needed you, but not five thousand dollars' worth.

As the shock wore off, he began to gather the remains of his strength, like tiny fragments of mercury, until the whole was there again. He made a small torch of splinters and searched the ground, finding a quantity of sulphur matches someone had dropped. And something else: the three-inch butt of a cigar.

Barksdale sat down and examined it.

It resembled a twist of thick, dried leather. He sniffed the tobacco. Rum-soaked. He could not recall ever having seen Breen smoke anything but cigarettes. As he sat pondering it, he noticed heel-prints in the damp earth among the fallen rocks. Bringing his torch close to the ground, he saw that some were small—cowboy boots—but others were wider. Town boots.

So there were two of them.

His mind ran back to the day of the coroner's hearing. *'Where were you before the hearing?'* he had asked Breen. *'I looked all over for you.'*

'I stayed in a room at the saloon . . .' Breen had said.

Right then he should have known! Should have dragged him off his horse and beaten his head in with a rock. Because right then, at that moment, Breen and Nacho Ruiz were cooking this up.

A flame of hope ran through him. Maybe the bastard hadn't left town yet! He might be waiting for that night train to Bisbee and points east. Scrambling to his feet, Barksdale headed up the tracks, stumbling so fast that he fell and the light was extinguished. He cursed, got to his feet, and blindly groped on, touching the wall for guidance like a blindman's cane. As he rounded the turn, the white glare of afternoon stabbed at his eyes from the tunnel entrance.

Forgetting caution, he ran for his horse.

So help me Christ, if I get my hands on you—! And if I don't, I'll beat the rotten liver out of your little Mexican buddy—

CHAPTER SIXTEEN

Until he was a half mile from the ranch, Logan did not attempt to talk to the Yaqui soldiers who formed his guard. He knew they had rigid orders, that when the fireplace was ripped out and the matter of his guilt settled, they would know exactly what to do.

The young warrior who was the leader of the group was called Basilio. He was tall, with dark features that might have been carved out of desert ironwood. His hair was cut in straight bangs below the brim of his hat. He seemed intelligent.

'It would be damned stupid,' Logan suddenly blurted, in Spanish. 'A murderer burying any of his loot under his own floor!'

'A man who is trusted may take unusual risks,' said Basilio.

'But under his own floor!'

Basilio pulled up on a ridge to gaze down on the ranch buildings. All the horses save Logan's were sweating: Yaquis were not horsemen. They transferred their uncertainty about animals to their mounts.

'A rancher may need money quickly, at times,' said the Yaqui.

'To buy supplies for his friends, the Yaquis,' Logan retorted. 'I disown my friends. My dead father would disown them.'

Basilio continued to peer down at the ranch. Logan's father had built his stronghold with an eye to trouble. The hill closest to the house was too low to provide a clear view of the roof across the parapets of the rear walls, which were higher than those in front. Only if a man stood up could he be seen. Evidently Manuela took seriously the matter of security, for Logan could see no sign of her.

Basilio made a hand signal. They rode down through the sparse growth to the ranch yard.

Tight-lipped, Logan dismounted. He waited until the others had gathered about him, then he walked wearily toward the house. A curiously detached feeling of compassion swept him: sympathy for a young rancher working hard and trying to mind his own business, who stepped in a trap too cruel to escape. He did not think it was self-pity, precisely. But he was dangerously close to feeling sorry for himself as he envisioned the moments ahead.

As he opened the door, he listened for sounds from the roof. Unless she had already fled, Manuela was following his orders and remaining silent.

Inside the big main room, the Yaquis stood looking about with quick, nervous motions. They reminded him of animals that had never seen the inside of a house.

'Where is the kitchen?' snapped Basilio.

Logan walked across the room to a door at the right. He gestured. '*Páse*,' he said. Basilio spoke to one of the soldiers, who went in rifle barrel first and could be seen peering about the small room. The man tilted his head. Basilio prodded Logan inside.

They all stood gazing at the small corner fireplace.

It swelled from the walls in a rounded half-barrel shape. There was a low hearth of adobe bricks and a small opening. Logan turned to the sink, started to pick up a stout butcher knife lying there, but thought better of it.

'*Cuchillo*,' he said, indicating the knife. Basilio murmured, '*Gracias*,' and tossed the knife butt first to one of the soldiers. Logan was amused at the polite turn things had taken. Maybe I'll get an *Excuse me* when they disembowel me, he thought.

Kneeling before the fireplace, the Yaqui scraped out the ash and half-burnt kindling.

'Look—there wasn't a real fire burned in it,' Logan pointed out. 'They just burned some kindling to cover the marks of digging.'

Basilio squatted to watch the work progress.

With the ash removed, the hearth was revealed as a scorched base of grayish fire-bricks. Using the knife point, the Yaqui commenced digging, removing ash from the mortarless joints. Logan sat on a chair to watch the work, feeling tense but fatalistic. One by one, the bricks came out. Two of the soldiers crowded closer to peer into the rectangular space. Basilio remained near Logan with the rifle on him.

The man who was digging made an exclamation. He reached into the space beneath the bricks and worked some earth aside. Then he lifted out a buckskin sack with rawhide drawstrings. He twisted to look at Basilio. He shook the sack and there was a dull rattle of coins. He spread the throat of the purse and upended it.

A handful of gold pieces jingled onto the floor.

Logan leaned back in the chair. Though he had expected it, he felt a dull shock of defeat. The Yaqui used his fingertip to flip the coins aside, one by one, as he counted them.

'Twenty-five,' he announced.

Twenty-five *reales* were worth about two hundred and fifty dollars. Someone was being mighty parsimonious with his life: should have brought at least five hundred, it seemed to him.

Basilio walked from his place to kneel beside the fireplace. Handing his rifle to one of the men, he returned the coins to the bag, and shoved it into a shirt pocket. Rising, he recovered his rifle and faced Logan. There was a long, throbbing silence. Logan was not afraid of the rifle: that would not be a hard death. He was afraid of the word which would bring out the knives.

He saw Basilio's thumb tighten on the knurled hammer of his rifle. It clicked off-cock. The Indian lowered the gun but continued to stare at him with his hard, black gaze.

'You are to find the men—Barksdale and Breen,' he said. 'You are to bring them to us at the same place. You are to find the money and bring it, also.'

Logan raised his hands, drenched with a weakness of relief. 'How can I do all that? Maybe I can bring their bodies, or have them arrested for investigation, but—'

'An investigation would bring posse men, and people who know nothing of our war. We have stayed too long already. By tomorrow night, we must leave.'

'What about the prisoners?' Logan protested.

'The prisoners will go with us.'

'It's no fault of theirs that—'

'It is no fault of ours that the kin were murdered. If you find the money later, and bring us the murderers, perhaps the prisoners can be brought back some day.'

*   *   *

Logan waited, sprawled in a deep chair on the gallery, drinking Mexican brandy. He gazed across the hills patterned with slanting late-afternoon shadows. Relief left him feeling slightly drunk. He savored his moment of relaxation. The job ahead was simple, in one sense. When he found Barksdale and Breen—if he could catch them out of town—he would settle with them quickly and with no more fuss than a single shot apiece. But in another sense, the job was complex.

How could he learn where the money was cached—if indeed it were still around—after he killed them?

Nacho Ruiz was another big card to play. Barksdale couldn't write a copperplate hand like that note in violet ink, and Breen was probably illiterate. So Nacho had written the note, as Pistola had all but admitted. But the three of them made a curious team, and he could hardly imagine them sitting down to agree on something like murder. Breen was a simple child of murderous impulse; Nacho a nasty-minded schemer and whoremaster; Barksdale was a two-fisted man of action and greed. It must have all started with Barksdale, who knew the Yaquis' habits. So perhaps that was the place to start in attempting to unwind the snarl.

The Yaquis had left his guns on the porch. He holstered his Colt after making sure they had not unloaded it; he opened the breech of the rifle. Then he went into the house and made some sandwiches of the black, coarse bread he had learned to bake after his father's death. He carried them, wrapped in old newspapers, to the back wall of the house.

'Manuela!' he called. 'They've gone.'

In a few moments the young woman's frightened face showed above the parapet.

'You did just right,' he said. 'Here's a sandwich for you. You'll have to stay up there again tonight.'

'Did you see Chaparro? What have they done to him?'

'He's all right. I'm still working on it, and I'll have to ride to Barksdale's, maybe to Nogales, now. Here—catch—'

He tossed the package to her. She caught it before it fell back. 'Stay out of sight,' he said. 'Don't show yourself. I don't know when I'll be back, but if I don't show up in a couple of days, try to make your way to town. Watch out for Barksdale and Joe Breen.'

'Go with God, Señor Logan.'

The light had failed by the time he reached Barksdale's ranch. He left his horse in a sandy wash a quarter-mile from the cabin and continued afoot. No lamp burned. The horses in the freighter's wedge-shaped horse trap moved restlessly as he passed. They had evidently not been fed today; this was a bad sign, dynamiting his hope of finding the man home. Nevertheless, he proceeded cautiously. The horses killed any chance of surprising Barksdale, as they paced along the smooth wire fence, following him and hoping for a few forkfuls of hay.

Coming in view of the mean little box-shaped ranch house, he lay in the weeds to reconnoiter. It was possible that Barksdale had heard his hoof sounds, extinguished the lamp, and set himself to wait. He was as sharp as an Indian. With time so short, Logan could not risk hurrying. On the other hand, he could not afford to wait. He lay there for fifteen minutes, listening to the click of insects in the brush, the restless stirring of the horses. Bats squeaked in the air, a marauding owl sat on the ridge pole of the cabin and uttered its unnerving cries, trying to frighten Manuela's hens from cover.

At last he rose and moved quietly toward the cabin, his spur rowels stilled with matchsticks. He was convinced that Barksdale was away. He knew his horse, and it was not in the corral or the horse trap. Stepping onto the porch, he moved close to the wall and listened again. He reached out and took hold of the white porcelain doorknob. He twisted it and threw the door open.

The cabin exhaled a breath of sour pipe tobacco, of stale food. But there was not a sound. Still, that black rectangle troubled him. If the freighter *were* inside, it was the door of death. He squinted, his heart pounding. A thought came. If someone had to go through it, why not Barksdale?

After a moment he ran to Chaparro's shack. The door was broken. He struck a match and looked about until he found some dish towels and a coal-oil lamp. He unscrewed the cap from the lamp and saturated the rags with oil.

Then he returned to the cabin and crouched before the gallery. After rolling the towels loosely, he struck a match and ignited one corner of the roll. He waited until the feeble blue flame grew yellow, shook out a little more of the oil-soaked rag, and hurled it into the cabin.

In a few seconds the door and the windows were illuminated by blue-and-yellow witch's light. Inside the cabin, he could see a table beginning to burn: the rags had rolled beneath it, the flames rising to scorch the edges of the dry wood. The fire grew, rising toward the ceiling of mesquite beams and small branches supporting the earthen roof.

He decided it might help to spread the fire if he shattered the table with a bullet. He aimed and fired a shot. Ripped by the bullet, the table flew against the back wall. In a few seconds a cot was in flames; some clothing hanging from a nail caught fire.

He watched in a joyful rage as the fire spread. The beams were catching; the frame of a window began to smolder. He ducked, startled, as a salvo of shots blazed out through the door. He could hear bullets stinging the air as he rolled toward a creosote shrub for shelter.

Then he realized it was only a box of ammunition which had been ignited by the flames. He ran behind Chaparro's shack, gathered up newspapers and kindling, and started a fire on the table. He poured cooking oil on the fire. It was blazing hotly when he ran out.

In the horse trap, he heard the animals running silently. From the cabin, there was a muffled thunder and a shower of sparks: a portion of the roof had fallen in. Smoke and dust billowed through the windows and door.

He walked back for his horse. At the foot of the horse trap, he opened the lower gate to let the animals out.

CHAPTER SEVENTEEN

The air was warm and dusty in the last hour before nightfall when Clyde Barksdale rode into Nogales. Merchants were closing their shops; a nostalgic fragrance of charcoal fires from the Mexican quarter filled the air with a special bordertown magic. For Barksdale, the lazy hour was a barb which tore his flesh with angry pain, reminding him of his plans, now hanging by a thread.

El Rancho Grande. That was what he had intended to call his ranch, back there when he quit freighting. He used to tell people a rancher was just a farmer with his brains knocked out. Now, he knew his mistake, but he also knew the remedy.

A ninety-dollar-a-month foreman.

The world paid little for savvy: it paid a lot for capital. He could have hired the best foreman in southern Arizona for ninety a month—fifteen dollars over the going rate—and with that ten thousand he could have stocked his ranch with shorthorns. He could have gotten a professor of animal husbandry down from the state college once a year to tell him which heifers to keep, which bulls to retain, which animals to throw in the beef herd.

This plan of his he had put together over the years. It was a sound one, too, and the only reason it had not worked was that he had not followed it. He had sunk all his cash in his poor man's ranch and left himself in the same position as people like Logan and Laura Sutton, living from crop to crop, borrowing on prospects.

The heel of his fist hit his big Chihuahua saddlehorn. He touched the flanks of his horse with the spurs and rode on through a scattered residential district. Near the center of town he walked the horse into the alley at the far end of which was the rear of the International

Saloon. Halfway down the block was a livery barn where Joe Breen usually stabled his horse. Barksdale dismounted and walked into the fragrant gloom of the barn.

Glancing at each horse in the double line of stalls, he approached the front. A couple of hostiers were forking up hay. Steve Lund, the stableman, was smoking a pipe in the doorway. Barksdale halted beside him.

'How's it going, Steve?' he asked.

Lund, a weathered old man with a seamed, dark face, glanced at him. 'Reckon I'll make it, Clyde,' he said. 'Still riding that bay horse I sold you?'

'Sometimes. Why?'

'I was thinking last time I saw you on him that maybe he wasn't horse enough to carry a big man. I've got a Morgan coming in that'd be just right for you.'

'You old swindler,' Barksdale chuckled. 'He must be sick, or you wouldn't bring the subject up. The reason I don't ride the bay much is that he goes sore-footed unless I keep carpet slippers on him.'

'You don't say!' The other man frowned. 'He was in perfect condition when you bought him. You tried him out, I recall.'

Barksdale punched his shoulder. 'But you were keeping sawdust in his stall so that his ringbone wouldn't hurt till he'd been rode a while, weren't you?'

'Clyde, I swear—' the old man began,

piously.

Barksdale laughed. 'Go to hell, you old horse-thief. Has Joe Breen been in town today?'

'Breen? God, lemme think. Breen. I don't think so.'

'You don't think . . . ?'

'No; he ain't been in. It's kind of unusual, too. He usually spends more time at the poker table than he does chousing cattle.'

Barksdale frowned. 'You're right. That's why I asked. I feel kind of responsible, because I recommended him to the Sutton girl. Decided I'd better speak to him. If you see him, send a boy to find me. Will you do that? I'll be around town a while.'

The stableman said he would. Barksdale walked back through the barn. One of these days, he thought, you'll buy that bay back from me, Lund, and you'll pay twice what I paid. But there's no hurry about that.

If the old man had not seen Breen in town, then there was a good chance that he had not come in. Barksdale felt a moment's bleak despair. On the other hand, there was still Nacho, and a chance that Breen was holed up at the saloon, waiting for train time tonight. That was a couple of hours yet—maybe three.

He left his horse at the stable and strolled down to the International Saloon. Glancing across the half-doors, he saw that the room was crowded. He did not spot Nacho immediately, and again there was a quake of rage and fright in his guts. *You sons of bitches—!* he thought—and then he saw the banty-rooster, Ruiz, in a brown suit, walking through the tables laying a Judas hand on this shoulder and that as he passed . . .

Barksdale found a spot at the bar.

A bartender came and took his order for a shot of whiskey. The freighter kept his head down, studying some coins he laid on the bar, but observing from the corner of his eye as Nacho reached the back-bar and spoke to a waiter. Nacho's plump brown features glistened with an exhilaration Barksdale had not seen there before. Every gesture and expression gave him away. He strolled to a display of bottles against the back-bar mirror, selected one, and carried it to the bar. There was a moment's banter as he poured a drink. Nacho refused the man's money for some reason, and returned the bottle to its place.

Then he faced the front of the saloon. His glance collided with Barksdale's. Almost physically he reacted; he controlled himself, gave the freighter a nod, and started to turn back.

'Hey, Nacho—got a minute?' Barksdale called.

'Why, sure, amigo,' Nacho replied. Bold as brass, he came to lay his palms on the edge of the counter and smile into Barksdale's eyes. '*Que tal?*' he asked.

Funny how, when he was nervous, he lapsed into real *poche* language, Barksdale thought. He spun one of the coins.

'Listen, I'm hunting Joe,' he said. 'Seen him around?'

'Joe Breen?'

'Yeah. Joe Breen.'

'No, I ain' seen him. I'll tell him you're lookin', though, if I see him.'

'Good. Oh, Nacho—' The man was turning away as Barksdale called him back. 'Got a cigar on you?'

Nacho frowned; he tilted his head toward the cash register. 'Any kind you want, Clyde. John will take care of you.'

'No—I mean one of your own.'

'My own?' Nacho gave a nervous chuckle. 'What's the joke, Clyde?'

'No joke. I saw you smoking one of them little rum-soaked kind the other day, and somebody told me you had them made special in Mexico City.'

'Somebody was kidding you.' From the breast pocket of his coat, the saloonkeeper drew two cigars. Round and plump as sausages, they were the pale green color of good tobacco. 'The fellow who told you that must have been rum-soaked, Clyde,' he laughed.

Barksdale was slightly stunned, having been positive that Nacho was the other man in the plot. He still thought so, as Nacho walked off.

No reason Nacho couldn't smoke a different kind of cigar once in a while.

When Barksdale was on his second whiskey, Nacho returned. He held a small chunk of ice in his hand, which he was palming back and forth as though washing his hands with it.

'I asked one of the boys about Joe, and he said he was in earlier. He's rode out to the ranch. I guess I missed him.'

A flame leaped high in Barksdale's head. He could hardly keep it from shining in his eyes.

'Well, hell,' he said, feigning chagrin. 'Reckon I missed him, then. I'll ride by Miss Sutton's on the way home. Thanks, Nacho.'

' 'Nada,' said Nacho.

A few minutes later Barksdale left.

* * *

A smoky dusk had drifted over the town. He strolled slowly, considering Nacho's lie. Nacho wanted him out of town: that was clear. Why? Was he hiding Breen? Was one of them planning to get on that Bisbee train tonight? Or were both?

He halted, smiling as he gazed up the street. Yes, sir! That was it. Something was stewing on the back lid of the stove, and he was one cook too many.

He followed a cross-street to the railroad yards, a dusty wedge of open land between two long blocks of adobe buildings. Crossing a set of tracks, he placed himself near a dripping water tower and surveyed the yard. A single set of tracks came up from Mexican Nogales and passed the station before splitting into a system of switches and turns. A line of ore cars waited to be picked up; a baggage truck loaded with express parcels sat before the small yellow station building. Lamps were burning inside the office and the waiting room, and a workman was lighting the red and green switch lamps.

Barksdale started down the tracks, his boots crunching in the coarse gravel. Reaching the station building, he studied the empty benches, the lighted office. He could see Harry Drew, the stationmaster, going through bills of lading at a counter.

He walked to a blackboard hanging against the rough adobe wall. Under the painted legend, *Eastbound,* was the figure, 9:10, and the chalked notation, *On time*. The eastbound came up from Sonora, dropped passengers and express, and headed on east along the border to Bisbee and the mining towns.

Nine-ten. He glanced through the dusty windows at the station clock. It was not quite seven. Two hours—but at least he knew now where to wait.

Turning, he saw the baggage truck piled with express and a few pieces of luggage. He walked over to the thin-wheeled cart and studied the bags. What kind of bag would I pick if I was shipping fifty pounds of gold? he wondered. A cow-hide valise caught his eye. He moved another bag and gripped the handle.

A man spoke sharply from the door. 'Hey! Stay away from that truck!'

Barksdale turned. Harry Drew stood in the open door, staring out at him. As the light fell on Barksdale's face, Drew recognized him and his manner changed.

'Oh—excuse me, Clyde. Help you?'

'I've got a box coming from Bisbee. I was just—'

'That's all outgoing stuff. Nothing's come for you.'

'All right. Thanks.' He sauntered off, and Drew closed the door.

As soon as he was in the shadows, the freighter headed for the water tower. The damp ground about it was white with alkali. A variety of pest weeds thrived in the hard earth, cresting a rough hedge about the base of the big wooden tank on its creosoted stilts. Barksdale peered up and down the tracks, then walked under the tank, found a dry plank to sit on, and made himself comfortable for the long wait. Before train time, Nacho would probably make a quick tour of the town to make sure Barksdale had left for the Sutton ranch. Barksdale wanted him and Joe to feel perfectly relaxed when they got aboard that train—a minute or two before he followed him.

CHAPTER EIGHTEEN

'Don't unsaddle him—I may be leaving soon,' Logan told Steve Lund.

'What's your hurry?' asked the stableman.

'I'm looking for a couple of people. Seen Clyde Barksdale?'

'Why, hell, that's his horse in the back stall. He was looking for somebody, too.'

'Who?'

Lund slipped a halter onto the horse and led it into a stall. 'Joe Breen.'

Logan waited in a breathless tension. 'He must not have found him, if he's still in town.'

'Reckon not.'

Logan waited again, decided Lund was not going to elaborate, and started for the street. He halted to glance at the clock on the wall of Lund's office: ten to nine. Reaching the sidewalk, he heard the hoot of a train whistle from Mexican Nogales—the mixed train from Sonora was making up for the run to Bisbee.

He started down the street, trying to decide exactly what he intended to do. He had no clear idea of where to start. He needed three men and ten thousand dollars. One of those men might be able to tell him where the money was, but no one could help him deal with them. Sheriff Mooney could do no more than arrest them—if that. For Mooney's law would not permit him to deliver them into Pistola's hands for Yaqui justice.

He flexed his fingers as he walked, eager for action. He decided Nacho Ruiz was the weakest link in the chain Barksdale had forged. There was a good chance, however, that he would run into Barksdale at the saloon. He turned down the side of a building to the alley in the rear. The last time he had entered the saloon from the rear, it had brought him good luck.

Opening the saloon's mosquito-bar door, he listened. The dim entry hall was quiet; three small whiskey kegs in the shadows waited to be carried out, a couple of cases of bottles beside them. From beyond the curtains he heard voices and a steady tinkle of glassware. He walked to the curtain, parted it, and glanced into the room.

Big, underlighted, and smoky, it did not reveal its secrets at once. Gradually he made out the crowded tables and the bar, a long line of men's backsides protruding as they stood hipshot, one boot on the railing. As the faces of the customers became clear, he searched for Barksdale, Breen, or Nacho. Waiters in tubular white aprons moved about the tables, carrying small round trays on upturned palms. After a full minute's scrutiny, he became convinced that none of the men was in the room. From far off, the muffled sound of a train whistle came: the night train was leaving for Bisbee.

He turned to gaze up the stairs. Nacho had his living quarters up there somewhere. The narrow stairs were illuminated by a lamp hanging at the first landing. He rubbed his palms on his thighs; finally he started up the stairs, the worn treads creaking under his boots.

Upstairs, a door closed with a solid thud.

He waited, his hand on the backstrap of his gun. Footfalls sounded overhead, turned, and now a man was descending the stairs. Logan drew his gun and waited. The tread was light and hurried, almost woman-like, except that it sounded too heavy and without any heels. The man reached the landing and turned to descend to the hall.

It was Nacho.

Seeing Logan, he stopped with one foot extended downward. He drew his foot back, smiled waxily, and seemed to flinch inside his natty brown suit.

'Oh, how's—what's new, *amigo*?' he asked.

Logan started up the stairs. 'Too much new to talk about here, Nacho,' he said. 'Where's your room?'

'Up here. But I got to see somebody right quick. Why don't you come on up and wait? Or I'll set you up with a drink downstairs.'

'I'll come up.'

Nacho wet his lips and cleared his throat. Logan stopped three steps below him. Nacho was shaking.

'What's the idea of the gun, *compadre*? I thought you was just kidding.'

'Turn around and climb,' said Logan.

After a moment Nacho started back up the stairs. 'Don't try to draw on me, either,' Logan said. 'I've had a bellyful of your tricks already.'

Nacho led him to a door at the end of the upstairs hall. Logan had him face the wall while he searched for weapons; he found a shoulder gun, and took it from him. 'Let's go inside,' he said.

Digging a key from his pocket, the saloonkeeper unlocked the door. Logan took a lamp from a wall bracket and carried it inside. He kicked the door shut and set the lamp on a table. Returning to the door, he moved the little night latch to the lock position.

'Light all the lamps you can find,' he ordered.

Nacho muttered, but set about lighting the four lamps in the room. The bed was neatly made, a few objects were laid out on the marble dresser top. The heavy drapes were closed.

'Sit down.' Logan gestured with the gun, then groped in his pocket. He dropped a slip of paper on Nacho's lap. The man glanced at it and looked up, bewildered.

'I don't get the joke!' he said.

Logan backhanded him across the mouth. 'You wrote it! And you're going out with me and tell Pistola why. Who's in this with you?'

Nacho wiped his mouth on his sleeve. 'In what, Tommy? I don't know what you're—'

'Don't "Tommy" me, Goddamn it!' Logan shouted. 'Where's your cut of the money?'

Trembling, Nacho put his hands together in a semblance of praying. 'Tom—I swear by the Holy Mother there's not a nickel in this room that isn't my own!'

'Then where is it?'

'I never had it! You mean that Yaqui money? I know nothing—'

Logan backhanded him again. Then, swearing, he walked to a closet door and opened it. He held a lamp inside and pulled all the clothes off the hangers onto the floor. He swept everything from a shelf with one arm. He searched the floor among pairs of Mexican boots with elastic tops. He found nothing.

He went back and sank his fingers into Nacho's shoulder. 'Don't tell me you didn't write that note, because I've seen the same violet ink on the spike by your cash register. Where's the money?'

Again Nacho prayerfully raised his hands. 'Tommy—'

Heavy footsteps ascended the stairs. Logan listened. The man was in a hurry.

'Who's coming?' he whispered.

'I don't know . . .'

The footfalls turned and came down the hall. Logan touched the back of Nacho's neck with the muzzle of his Colt.

'If he comes to the door; let him in. Make sure he comes inside. Say one damn word about me, and you're a dead saloonkeeper.'

Nacho shuddered and moved forward to escape the pressure of the gun. Someone tried the knob. Then a deep, angry voice said:

'Ruiz! Hey, open up—!' It was Clyde Barksdale.

'Let him in—'

Logan walked to the closet, eased the door closed, and squatted on the floor among the boots. If it were opened, he wanted that first shot to go high.

He heard Nacho open the door. Then there was a sound of scuffling, a blow struck, and the saloonkeeper's cry. A man fell to the floor.

'You bastardly—where's the money?' Barksdale shouted.

Nacho began denying everything. Then his voice caught.

'Clyde, for Christ's sake—!' he gasped.

'It's as sharp as your sideburns, too,' Barksdale said. 'It'll cut greasy skin like yours without a whisper. You know what I'm going to do to you, don't you?'

'Listen, Clyde!—Joe Breen—'

'I'm going to scalp you. What about Breen?' Barksdale demanded.

'He's got the money,' Nacho panted. 'He

was going to take off tonight.'

'From where?'

'The ranch. He was laying low today, and tonight he was going to leave. Just ride out—head north—'

Then his voice tightened, and he gasped, 'Oh, Jesus, no—no, listen—!'

Logan heard a scuffling. 'I'm bleeding!' he heard Nacho cry.

Barksdale chuckled. 'You better believe you're bleeding, Mex. The cut's only an inch long, though, right at your hairline. I'll take it all the way around, if I have to. So that's where Breen's cut of the money's going. Now, how about yours?'

'It's gone!'

'Come on—you can do better than that. Gone where?'

'Gone to Bisbee, on the train. I was going to be on the train too . . .'

'That's what I figured. Why weren't you?'

'I got held up, Clyde. That's God's truth. A—a guy came here. I couldn't run him out without him getting suspicious. The bag will be held for me at Tucson. I checked it through. I was going to transfer from Bisbee to Tucson—'

'In whose name?'

'Mine. The ticket's—here it is, in my vest pocket. Baggage check, too.'

There was a pause, then Barksdale's rumbling voice. 'Well, you got one truthful word in you, at least. What's the story about

Breen, now?'

'God's truth, Clyde! We got worried. You see, Joe came to me one day, said you and him had this gold hid out—he was only getting a third of it—so he'd split even with me if I helped him.'

'Helped him what? Why didn't he just walk off with it?'

'Well—'

Barksdale laughed. 'Write me a letter about it, Nacho. About how you seen us killing the Indians and put the pressure on him to split with you. Ain't that about how it went? I don't think Joe has sense enough to double-cross a man.'

Nacho giggled. 'I guess so, Clyde—'

There was a cry, quickly muffled; then a deep, prolonged groan. Logan heard Barksdale's spurs, chime as he rose. But from Nacho, he heard only long moaning cries.

'You ain't hurt,' Barksdale said. 'Just tell the doc you cut yourself shaving.'

'Clyde, I—I'm crucified! Holy Mary—'

'I'd join you in your devotions,' said Barksdale, 'excepting I've got to take Breen's trail. He ain't been tracked until he's been tracked by me. I'll take these tickets and pick up the rest of it later. If I was you, I'd forget anything ever happened here.'

A moment later the door closed. Nacho continued praying, then called, in a faint voice:

'Logan! Help me, Tommy—'

Logan found him lying on his back with his knees drawn up, his shoulder pinned to the floor by the freighter's bone-handled knife.

*   *   *

The blade had passed through the muscles on the outside of Nacho's shoulder before entering the plank. Barksdale had pulled his coat open and driven the knife point through his ruffled silk shirt. The saloonkeeper could not move without agony. His hand hovered about the haft of the knife, but he seemed afraid to touch it.

'How about it?' Logan asked. 'Has Breen really left?'

Closing his eyes, the tears squeezing from under the lids, Nacho began to weep. His free hand pounded the floor in agony. 'Joe was leaving the ranch tonight. I guess he's already gone. Oh, God! Help me, Logan, help me!'

'Where was he going?'

'I don't know. Just going. Logan, please—you don't know—'

'Sure, I know. I know who wrote that note to Pistola, too. Do you know what they'd have done to me? It wouldn't be hard to guess, would it? But that didn't worry you.'

Nacho's eyelids fluttered open. 'Ain't you worried about Barksdale getting the money from Joe and taking off?'

'Not a damn bit. Because I know how to

track too. And I'll track them both clear to hell if I have to.'

He turned and glanced about. Nacho made a feeble gesture toward the knife. 'Tommy, I think I'm bleeding to death,' he said weakly.

'You aren't bleeding much.' Logan opened the closet again, and picked up a low boot with a flat heel. He went to one knee beside Nacho, who regarded him in puzzlement. 'Close your eyes,' he said. 'This'll pain you a little.'

When Nacho closed his eyes, he struck the haft of the knife solidly with the heel, driving the blade another inch into the floor. Nacho cried out, then opened his eyes.

'Can I move, now?' he asked.

Logan shrugged and rose. 'That's up to you. You're still crucified, amigo. If I were you, I'd stay there till Sheriff Mooney brought the doctor. I'll pass the word before I leave. But I wouldn't feel right with you running around loose, and nothing settled yet. You can understand that, can't you?'

He walked to the window as the saloonkeeper broke into hysterical pleading, cursing, and weeping. Glancing into the alley, he saw a man leave the rear of the saloon and walk north. Barksdale, without doubt—but no hurry. The easiest way to get him where he wanted him was to let him ride there, unfettered.

CHAPTER NINETEEN

Joe Breen had found a pair of exceptionally fine saddlebags in a trunk in the bunkhouse. At nine-thirty, everything else ready, he packed them with his share of the gold. Handcarved, the leather bore a pattern of imaginative flowers and vines, with the initials, *A. S.* in the center of an oval shield. Alden Sutton—in memory of a greenhorn.

After dividing the money with Nacho, he had spent the day going through the motions of working, just in case Barksdale should drop in to ask him to ride up to the mine and make the split. In that case, he would have had to kill him and leave him in the mine.

But all had gone smoothly. He had come in at dark, told the Sutton wench things looked fine over in the Flat Rock pasture. Then he teased the Mexican cook, Lucha, out of a stack of tortillas, several cakes of Mexican goat cheese, and a little sack of brown-sugar *piloncillos*. He should reach a town before he needed any more food.

Now that everything was moving, he felt a sense of exhilaration. He thought of the girls of El Paso, with their creamy complexions and black hair brushed to the lustre of a crow's wing . . . Next he was thinking about Laura Sutton, and frowning toward the ranch house as he lifted the heavy saddlebags in place behind the cantle of his saddle.

Damned shame to go away without sampling the merchandise, he thought. But then he thought of the Indians . . . The important thing at this point was to get the hell out of the area, he decided.

He went back to the bunkhouse. And, as he entered it, there she was, standing beside his cot, looking puzzled. All that lay on the cot was a blanket roll tied with leather straps.

'Joe? What on earth—!' she said.

'Oh, uh-didn't I tell you?' he said. 'I'm going in town for a couple of days. Stuff's been piling up that I got to tend to.'

'Stuff?' the girl said, dubiously. The lamplight brushed her face with warm yellow tones.

'Personal stuff,' said Breen. And a certain urge in him stretched luxuriously, like a rooster on a corral bar. '*You* know,' he said, with a lift of his shoulders, beginning to smile boldly at her.

She saw the look in his eyes, and he observed the way her eyes fell and her mouth tightened. 'Oh—well, it's up to you,' She said. 'Just so you're back before—too long.'

She started for the door. To reach it, she had to pass him. Breen stretched his arm across the aisle between the posts and planted his palm against one of the wing supports. She stopped abruptly, looking down.

'Let me by,' she said.

'Hey,' Breen said softly. 'What'd you come out here for?'

'To ask where you were going. Why else?'

'How'd you know I was going anywhere?'

'Lucha told me you'd asked for some things.'

'Why didn't you send Lucha to find out?'

'Why should I have?'

Breen put his finger under her chin and tipped her face up. 'You know, I never figured you for that kind,' he murmured.

She pushed at his arm, but he stood fast. 'Let me by!'

'Ain't you got an urge too, Miss Laurie?' he asked.

Laura swung openhandedly at his face. Then, when she tried to duck past, he caught her by the waist and brought her against him. She screamed. He started kissing her, but she bit his cheek and he pushed her away and slapped her. As she tried to run, sobbing, he caught her again and threw her down on the cot. His hand forced her back until she was lying crosswise, staring up at him. She opened her mouth to scream again.

Lifting the blanket roll, Breen jammed it down over her face. He sat straddling her, holding the blankets over her mouth until her striking became a panicky threshing.

'Any time you want to quit—' he panted. 'Won't take long, lady.'

Suddenly, with a gunman's instinct, he knew someone had entered the bunkhouse. He did not turn his head, knowing that was the fatal trigger he must not pull. Instead, he threw himself sideways on the cot and drew his gun . . .

* * *

Logan was a half mile from the ranch house when he heard the shots. There were four of them, evenly spaced. He touched his horse with the spurs, but the animal responded poorly. The horse had already carried him a day's travel since sunup. He held him to a jog. Approaching the ranch house, he heard hoof-beats to the west. He pulled up to listen. His impulse was to follow them. A sense of logic told him to find out what had happened at the ranch, first. He was sorry he had not taken time to take Laura into town; yet, if he had, he would have missed Nacho.

Riding in, he saw no lights, but heard women wailing in the main house. He looked for saddle horses. The yard was empty. 'Laura!' he shouted.

The wailing ceased. '*Laura!*' he called again. And then, '*Lucha! Qué pasa?*'

A casement. window flew open. A woman shrieked a few words of Spanish, asking who he was. He answered and rode closer. The woman gasped a few sentences.

'Señor Breen has been murdered! Señor Barksdale has taken the lady away. She was crying. He told her she was all right. But she screamed—'

'Where was he going? Do you know?'

The woman knew nothing but that Señor Breen had been most horribly murdered. Logan shouted that he would be back, and rode away.

The horses he had heard leaving were heading west. Nothing lay to the west but the foothills running to the railroad pass at Nogales. There were minor passes in the hills, and perhaps Barksdale was heading for one of them.

As he rode, Logan conjectured. Barksdale was in deep, and knew it. In deep with the law, but also with the Yaquis. In his place, I'd stay out of the hills, he thought. On the other hand, he had at least one murder to worry about now, and his best hope of safety lay in getting through the hills to one of the Mexican towns.

The farther west he rode, the less chance there was of running into Yaquis, because he would be closer to Nogales and its spreading civilization.

He rode the horse hard for a while, then reined up abruptly to listen. The silence seemed complete, except for the snorting of the horse. Then he heard crickets, like a thousand tiny bells of different pitch. The creaking of his saddle as the horse blew was an ominous factor; it told him the horse was nearly done.

Far off to the southwest, he heard the dash of hoofs against stone in some dry wash. Then again silence.

He spurred the horse. It tried to rear, brought its fore-hoofs down, and went into a ragged lope.

When he halted the animal again, he heard the steady *clop-clop* of hoofs not over a quarter mile away. He rubbed the sweaty withers of the horse, listening. Suddenly he drew his Colt and fired a shot into the air. The hoof sounds died an instant later.

Okay, you bastard! he thought. Think about that for a while. Slow down, now, and keep yourself covered . . .

A girl screamed.

He sank the rowels into the horse's flanks; it squealed and ran, tossing its head. He rode hard for a time, then pulled up. Again there was silence. He wondered whether Barksdale would dismount immediately on hearing the shot, or keep riding, trying to maintain his lead.

There was a hard clatter of hoofs, a shout, then a gunshot. The girl screamed again, and the hoof sounds kept coming. Logan leaped to the ground to sprawl behind a desert shrub. He was searching for a target when he heard Laura's voice.

'Tom!'

*   *   *

Huddled beside him on the ground, the girl told him what had happened. Logan put his arm around her shoulders.

'Where was he taking you?' he asked her.

'To Mexico. He didn't want me telling anyone what I'd seen, or what Joe had told me. Not until he was out of the country.'

'Did you see him kill Breen?'

She nodded, but she began weeping again when she tried to tell this part of the story.

Logan rose and picked up the reins of her horse. 'Is this your horse?' he asked

'It's Joe's. He was packing to leave when I discovered him. Barksdale put me on the horse after—after he killed Joe.'

Logan looked the horse over. It was a sound animal, carrying a fine saddle—Alden Sutton's initials were on the *sudaderos.* Sutton's saddlebags were lashed behind the cantle, too. He hit one, testing it. The feel and sound of it were solid. He unfastened the buckles and groped inside.

The horse ahead of him was moving again. He knelt beside Laura.

'I've got to stay with him. Take my horse and head back. He's about done, but he'll carry you. You don't have to be afraid—there's no one left who'd bother you.'

'I'm afraid, Tom! Barksdale told me to be

quiet—that the hills were full of Indians.'

'Indians are what I'm hoping for. If I can give them Barksdale tonight, you may never see another Indian outside of a railroad station. Don't worry about Yaquis.'

He brought the horse and helped her into the saddle. 'Go back and have some elderberry wine with Lucha,' he told her. 'It's wicked stuff, but it may get you over your nerves.'

She squeezed his hand. 'I won't get over my nerves until you come back.'

'That'll be soon.'

From the sounds, Barksdale was trying to work west before striking into the hills. The freighter knew the Yaquis' habits as well as Logan did—that they kept to the passes east of town. And he knew also that right now he was three or four miles west of the rincon where the Rurales had died.

The fresh horse was strong and responsive. As he took a new line due west across the apron of the hills, it hit into a level jog that ate up the distance. Presently he reined in and listened. He had gained a little on Barksdale, a heavier man riding a tired horse.

He drew his Colt and fired two shots in Barksdale's direction. The flashes illuminated the slope rising from his feet toward the high, dark scarps obscuring the sky. Echoes rolled back. A hushed stillness followed, broken suddenly by the vicious crack of Barksdale's rifle. The shot screamed off the ground. Logan fired once more, then rode hard to divert Barksdale from his western course and push him against the cliffs.

For fifteen minutes the contest continued. Against the sky, Logan could see a break in the hills which meant a high pass. Barksdale was making for the trail which led into it.

Abruptly, he saw the flash of a gun, then heard a reverberating thunder. The shot was high over his head, a desperate shot from close at hand. Dismounting, he took cover in some mesquite. He could hear Barksdale's horse moving slowly through the brush. The man was flanked now, but still coming.

Logan's horse whickered. Immediately Barksdale fired. The bullet ripped through the mesquite. Logan fired back. The shot must have come close, for he heard the freighter swear, then swerve his horse.

At last he heard what he had been waiting for: the sound of his horse swinging east, as Barksdale headed for the next passable trail through the mountains.

Logan mounted quickly and followed, riding hard for a short distance before stopping to listen. The hoof sounds were growing more distant. Barksdale was in flight, caring for nothing but a hole in the bag out of which he might squirm.

Once he started up a trail which Logan knew ended in a blind canyon. But in a short time the freighter, too, realized he was boxing himself in; he cut from the trail across the ridge to regain the main east-west trail.

Then, from far ahead, Logan heard what he had been praying for: the dry, hard thumping of a drum.

* * *

Almost immediately the sound of a horse loping came through the darkness—Barksdale, in panic, was riding toward the cliffs. But another drum, and still another, broke out near the base of the high cliffs. The horse halted, and in the silence Logan read a story of desperation.

In a moment the horse was running again, north this time toward the Sutton ranch. Again it stopped, as a Yaqui drum set up a resonant throbbing like the warning rattle of a snake. But it was only a hesitation this time; Barksdale quickly spurred the horse on toward the drums.

Suicide, Logan decided: 'Kill me, you bastards!' he was saying. 'Kill me—don't torture me!'

A gunshot blasted. The hoof sounds faltered, stopped, and a man cried out as the horse went down at full lope. Logan rode toward the sound of the action.

Barksdale's voice came, a pained bellow full of challenge.

'Come on, you sons of bitches! Try and get

me!'

The drums were rattling before he finished. They ringed him in a great, patient circle. Barksdale went running down the slope, his rifle blasting. The drums thudded but the guns were silent. Logan heard him fall and get up again. The man ran on, then came to a staggering halt. Logan pictured him standing on the earth with his boots set wide apart, trying to summon the courage to kill himself.

The drums never stopped. One by one, new ones joined in as the warriors were summoned by the ancient telegraph. Barksdale went stumbling on down the slope.

Logan hung back. It was not a game he wanted to play. He was sick; he was deadly tired. But he could not leave—or try to—without explaining to Pistola that he had delivered one of his prisoners and half his money, and had the best of intentions about the rest.

He fired a revolver shot. The drums went silent as the Yaquis appraised the sound. 'Pistola!' he shouted. *'Vén acá!'*

Waiting, he untied the rawhide thongs which secured the saddlebags. He dropped the heavy bags on the ground and sat beside them to wait. In the darkness, the drums were drifting farther from the trail. It might have been ten minutes that he sat there alone. Then he became conscious, by some special sense of his own, that a man stood behind him.

'*Amigo*,' he said.

'*Compadre!*' the chief growled. He came forward and squatted beside Logan.

'You have one of the men,' Logan said. 'Another is dead in the Sutton woman's bunkhouse. The *llori* is in Nogales with a knife through his shoulder. I don't know whether he'll go to jail or not. I don't know how I can bring him here, but I'll try.'

'Does not matter,' said the chief. 'Nacho cannot go far. There are many of the kin in Tucson. Sooner or later we take him, no? What is in the saddlebags?'

'About half the money, according to what I could learn. I haven't counted it. Barksdale's carrying a baggage check for the rest. If you bring me the check, I'll go to Tucson and take the money wherever you say.'

'*Bien*,' the chief said, accepting the compromise.

'Can I ride back now without having my throat cut?' Logan asked him.

The chief reached behind him and spoke two words. A soldier moved up and offered him a flat drum like the top of a small keg. Pistola thumped the drum and handed it to him.

'Here—your *salvo conducto*,' he said.

Logan got up. Weary, he leaned against the horse for a moment before mounting. He offered his hand; the chief accepted it.

'May the war go well,' Logan said.

'May yours go well, too. There is always a war, no? For treasure, freedom, or a woman.'

Carrying the drum under his arm, Logan turned the horse and started back across the foothills.

We hope you have enjoyed this Large Print book. Other Chivers Press or G.K. Hall & Co. Large Print books are available at your library or directly from the publishers.

For more information about current and forthcoming titles, please call or write, without obligation, to:

Chivers Press Limited
Windsor Bridge Road
Bath BA2 3AX
England
Tel. (01225) 335336

OR

G.K. Hall & Co.
295 Kennedy Memorial Drive
Waterville
Maine 04901
USA

All our Large Print titles are designed for easy reading, and all our books are made to last.